D0889692

OLD MISSION STORIES OF CALIFORNIA

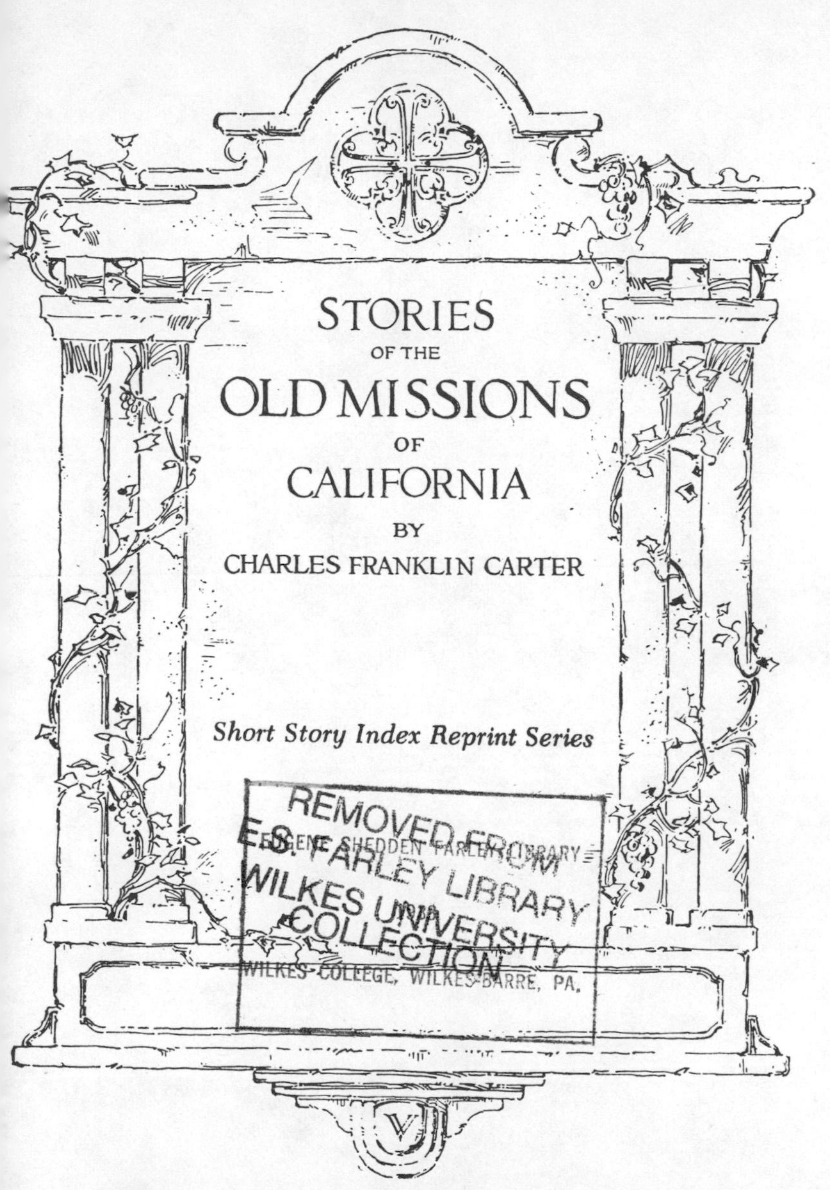

STORIES OF THE OLD MISSIONS OF CALIFORNIA

BY

CHARLES FRANKLIN CARTER

Short Story Index Reprint Series

BOOKS FOR LIBRARIES PRESS
FREEPORT, NEW YORK

First Published 1917
Reprinted 1970

STANDARD BOOK NUMBER:
8369-3447-4

LIBRARY OF CONGRESS CATALOG CARD NUMBER:
71-116945

PRINTED IN THE UNITED STATES OF AMERICA

CONTENTS

FOREWORD

Of the last six stories comprising the seven in this little collection of Stories of the Old Missions, all but one have, as a basis, some modicum, larger or smaller, of historical fact, the tale of Juana alone being wholly fanciful, although with an historical background. The first story of the series may be considered as introductory to the mission tales proper.

In these quiet, unpretending stories the writer has attempted to give a faithful picture of life among the Indians and Spaniards in Nueva California during the early days of the past century.

October, 1917.

THE INDIAN SIBYL'S PROPHECY

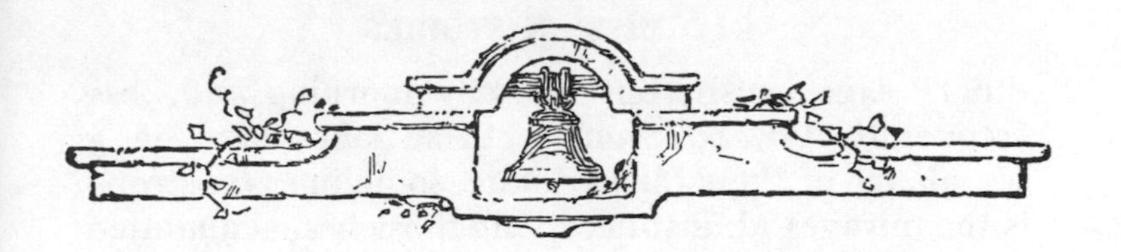

THE INDIAN SIBYL'S PROPHECY

IN THE southern part of the Mojave Desert a low hill stands somewhat apart from the foot-hills beyond, and back of it. Although not more than two hundred feet above the surrounding plateau, on account of its peculiar location, a commanding view may be had from its top. In front, toward the south, and extending all the way from east to west, the plain stretches off for many miles, until it approaches the distant horizon, where it is merged into lofty mountains, forming a tumultuous, serrated sky-line. Midway between the hill and the distant mountains, lie the beds, sharply defined, of three dry lakes. In the garish light of day they show for what they are, the light yellow hard-baked soil of the desert, without even the ordinary sage brush; but in early morning and, less frequently, toward evening, these lakes take on a semblance of their former state, sometimes (so strong is the mirage) almost deceiving those best acquainted with the region. Years ago—how many it would be difficult to say—these dry lakes were veritable bodies of water; indeed, at an earlier period than that, they were, without doubt, and including a large extent of the surrounding desert, one vast lake. But that was centuries ago, maybe, and with time the lake dried up, leaving, at last, only these three light spots in the view, which, in their turn, are growing smaller with the passing years, until they, too, will vanish, obliterated by the encroaching vegetation.

Back of the eminence from which this extended view is had, the mountains come close, not as high as those toward the south, but still respectable heights, snow-covered in winter. They array themselves in fantastic shapes, with colors changing from hour to hour. One thinks of the desert as a barren sandy waste, minus water, trees and other vegetation, clouds, and all the color and beauty of nature of more favored districts. Not so. Water is scarce, it is true, and springs few and far between, and the vegetation is in proportion; for what little there is is mostly dependent on the annual rainfall, never excessive, at the best, yet always sufficient for the brush covering the ground, and the yuccas towering up many feet here and there. But color, beautiful, brilliant, magnificent color, is here any and every day of the year, and from earliest dawn until the last traces of the evening sun have faded away, only to give place to moonlight unsurpassed anywhere in the world. Truly, the desert is far from being the dry, desolate, uninteresting region it is commonly pictured.

More than a century and a quarter ago, there stood on the side of this hill, and not far from its top, an Indian hut, or wickiup. It was built after the manner of the Indian tribes of Southern California—a circular space of about fifteen feet in diameter enclosed by brush-work, and roofed by a low dome of the same material. At the side was an opening, too small to permit one to enter without stooping low. This doorway, if it may be so called, being window and chimney as well, fronted toward the south, facing the dry lakes and the mountains beyond. Close by, at the left, was a heap of bones, which, on a nearer view, disclosed themselves to be those of rabbits, coyotes and quail, while three or four larger bones in the pile might inform the zoologist that the fierce mountain-lion was not unknown to this region. To the right of the doorway, some ten feet from it, were two large flat stones, set facing each other, a few inches apart; between them lay a handful of ashes, betokening the kitchen of the family living here. Close by the stones lay a number of smooth, rounded stones of use and value to the people of the hut. Back of the wickiup, a few paces up the hill, a tiny spring issued from the ground, affording a neverfailing, though scanty, supply of water.

The location of this solitary hut, remote from all other signs of humanity, so far as the eye could judge, was a singular one; for the Indian loves his kind, and it is rare that one wanders deliberately away to make his home in loneliness, far from the rest of the tribe to which he belongs. In the case of this hut, however, its solitariness was more apparent than real; for although out of sight of any habitation whatever, the tribe to which its inmates belonged was distant not more than two miles, but on the other face of the hill, and hidden far in the recesses of a small cañon. Here, on the site of a beautiful source of precious water, was a cluster of Indian houses of brush, built like the one on the hillside. Each had its fireplace on one side, as well as the accompanying heap of bones of animals killed in the chase. Near the centre of the group of huts stood the *temescal*—an institution with nearly every Southern California tribe of Indians—where those who were ill subjected themselves to the heroic treatment of parboiling over a fire, until in a profuse perspiration, to be followed, on crawling out, by a plunge into the icy water of the stream. It was truly a case of kill or cure.

Let us return to the hillside hut, and make the acquaintance of its inmates. Passing through the humble opening, the interior is disclosed to the curious eye at one glance. The ground embraced within the circle of the wickiup had been dug away so as to make an even, hard floor two or three feet below the surface of the earth outside. To the right, standing on the floor, were two large, round baskets, each one with a capacity of half a dozen gallons. They were made in conformity to the general type of basket of the Southern California aborigine, but with the distinctive marks peculiar to the tribe to which belonged the dwellers within, and woven so tightly as to hold water without permitting a drop to pass through. In the bottom of one of these baskets was scattered a little ground meal of the acorn, a staple article of food with all the Indians of California. The other basket, similar to the first in shape and size, but of rougher weave, and lined on the inside with bitumen, was nearly full of water; for though the finely woven baskets of the Southern California Indians were really water-tight, they were not generally used for liquids. Any one, acquainted with the customs of these Indians, would understand the meaning of the little heap of stones by the fireside without: they were used in warming the water in the basket, which was done by heating them in the embers of the fire, then, when hot, throwing them into the water, in this way bringing it almost to a boil. Afterward, the stones having been taken out, some meal was thrown in and, in this manner, cooked. Beyond the baskets, and nearly opposite the entrance, against the wall, was a heap of fine brush, covered with the tawny skin of an immense mountain-lion—a giant specimen of his species, and a formidable animal, truly, for an Indian to encounter with only bow and arrow.

On this bed of brush was the gaunt, emaciated form of a woman lying stretched out at full length. At first glance, one might have mistaken her for a mummy, so still and lifeless she lay; her face, too, carried out the resemblance startlingly, for it was furrowed and seamed with countless wrinkles, the skin appearing like parchment in its dry, leathery texture. Only the eyes gave assurance that this was no mummy, but a living, sentient body—eyes large, full-orbed and black as midnight, arched by heavy brows that frowned with great purpose, as if the soul behind and beyond were seeking, powerless, to relieve itself of some weighty message. These were not the eyes of age, yet they belonged to a countenance that gave token of having lived through a great many years; for the woman lying there so deathly still had experienced all the varied joys and sufferings of near four score years, each one leaving its indelible mark on the tell-tale face. She was clothed in a loose dress made from rabbit skins, sewn together coarsely, sleeveless, and so short as to leave her feet and ankles bare.

To the left of the entrance crouched a young Indian woman. She was an unusually good-looking specimen of the desert tribes: a tall well-shaped form; a head and face of much beauty and character, with a pair of eyes that, at first glance, betrayed a close relation to the woman lying on the bed. They were of the same size, color and brilliance; but the tense, powerful expression that was seen in those of the aged woman, here was softened to a mild, yet piercing glance, which had, at the same time, a touch of sadness. She appeared to be not more than twenty-five years old, although her face, in spite of its gentle, youthful expression, showed the traces of more than her full quota of hardships; for the life of the desert Indian is never an easy one at the best, and here had been a greater struggle for existence than is usual among the aborigines. As she crouched by the doorway, she seemed almost as lifeless as the old Indian woman on the bed, her gaze fixed absently on the extended view of plain and mountain stretching out before her, the only sign of life being the slow, even rise and fall of her bosom with each succeeding breath. Her dress was similar to that of the other woman, but was shorter, reaching only to the knees.

This young Indian was the granddaughter of the older woman. On the death of her parents (her father's following that of her mother, the daughter of the aged Indian, after an interval of a few months), when she was little more than an infant, her grandmother had taken sole charge of her, treating her, as she became older, with the closest intimacy, more as a sister than a grandchild; and notwithstanding the diversity in age, this feeling was reciprocated on the part of the child.

It was after her father's death, but before she herself was old enough to see more than the surface of action, that her grandmother took up her abode in the lone hut on the brow of the hill, apart from the rest of the tribe of which she was a member, with the child her only companion. At first, the little girl noticed not the difference between their mode of living and that of the rest of the tribe, all the other members of which lived together, surrounding the spring of water, their life and mainstay; but very quickly, as the child grew older, she saw, only too plainly, that her grandmother was looked upon as different from the others: and the Indian regards all those of his kin, no matter how near, who display any peculiar form of mentality, either with reverence, as something of the divine, or with cruel hatred, when he believes the unfortunate individual possessed with the evil spirit. She saw, in the brief and infrequent visits the two made to the tribe, that her grandmother was regarded with distrust; that glances of aversion were cast at her from the doorways of the huts as they passed, and, once or twice, a mischievous boy had slyly thrown a stone at the two, wending their way to their lonely home.

Long the child cogitated over the situation, but, as is the Indian's habit, without a word to her grandparent of what was occupying her mind. The old woman saw she was absorbed in some mental problem, and, with the shrewdness of the aborigine, guessed the subject, and sought to divert her thoughts into other channels. It was in vain, for one evening, after their simple meal of herbs, the girl, gathering courage, in the increasing dusk, asked abruptly, after a long silence:

"Grandmother, why do we live here alone, far from the others in the cañon? Why do we—?" she paused, frightened at her temerity.

The old woman started slightly. She had been sitting with hands folded quietly in her lap, thinking, possibly, of the absent ones of her family, gone to be with Ouiot in the everlasting home. Turning to her granddaughter, she answered, slowly and solemnly:

"My child, I am grieved to have this come upon you now, for I had hoped you would escape it until after I am gone to the eternal life beyond. Then it would not have been to you a burden, only a sorrow, softened by the thought that I had borne bravely the punishment dealt out to me, without a word of reproach. I have seen that you had something on your mind, and guessed this was it, and now that you have asked me, I think it best to tell you, although you are still but a child. For you would, I know, brood over it in your heart. Listen, then, while I tell you my life story.

"My childhood and youth were passed in a manner no different from that of the other children of our tribe; I worked and played, careless of everything but the present, until I was a big girl. I was happy in my ignorance, for why should I be singled out from all the rest to bear the honor that was to be thrust upon me? I knew not what was in store for me.

"One night, when I was about fifteen years old, I dreamed that the spring, near which our kindred live, dried up, and forced us to move to another spring where we had to stay for two months. When I came to myself (for it was not so much like sleep as a trance), I wondered; but this passed away after a time, and I had almost forgotten the occurrence, when one day, about a month later, we were startled by hearing there was no water in the spring. The winter before had been very dry, with almost no rain, and fears had been expressed that the spring would fail us, a thing which had not occurred for more than three generations. My dream flashed through my mind, only for an instant, but long enough to imprint the coincidence on my memory. I thought no more of it, however, until some six months later, after our return to the spring; for, as I saw it in my dream, we had been forced to depart, and to be absent from our beloved dwelling-place for two months. Again I saw, as in a dream (but this time it was full day, and I knew I was not asleep), our entire tribe in mourning for our chief who was lying dead and surrounded by all the elders. It was like a flash of lightning, leaving me, once more, broad awake, yet I had not been asleep. This time I was frightened, for I knew there had been members of our tribe who could foretell the future. Was I to be one of them? I dared not tell any one of my dream, and waited trembling, from day to day, hoping and praying that it might not come true. But the future had been revealed to me, and a few weeks later our chief fell in a battle with our enemies to the east. When I heard of it I swooned, and my mother found me lying senseless by the fire. After she had revived me, she asked me the cause of my fainting, and, weakened from the shock, I told her all.

"'Daughter,' she said, after a long pause, 'you are destined for a great work, for Ouiot speaks through you.' And, a few days later, after the burial of the dead, she told the chief men of the tribe what I had seen. And then ended my happiness: from that day I lived a life of sorrow, for the burden I had to bear was a heavy one: not only when I foretold disaster and suffering to our people, but when I had joyful news for them, even then the dread of knowing the future was terrible. Sometimes a half-year would pass without communication from above, and I would begin to hope that the awful gift was taken from me; but always it would manifest itself again. My husband (for I had been married not long after my first dream) left me just before your mother was born, but I did not want, for I was provided with everything by the entire tribe. Your mother, also, when she grew to be a woman, left me to be married to your father; but when he died, he asked me to take care of his only child, and that is why you and I have lived together all these years."

The old woman paused, and several minutes passed silently in the gathering dusk, while the little girl waited wonderingly, afraid to speak. Presently the Indian stirred, as if waking from a slumber, and, after a slight shiver, resumed her tale:

"And thus I lived for many years, prophesying as the Great Spirit revealed the future to me, and my prophecies always came true. I foretold poor harvests, and the issues of our wars. Only once before the last prophecy I made was my word doubted, and then unbelief was born in the minds of many of the men. I spoke the words of truth then, but when I said we should, in time, vanish from this country, I was treated with scorn. But I was right. Are we greater in numbers than our traditions tell us were our fathers many generations ago? Is it not more difficult to live now than it was in former days? Where are the quail, the rabbits, that our ancestors used to kill so plentifully? Are not they growing less all the time? And the water! Look—" and the old woman, with arm extended, pointed with her forefinger toward the three dry lakes in the distance, only one of which showed any signs of moisture, a small spot in the centre, covered with, perhaps, a foot of water—"look," she repeated, "what were those lakes years ago? Our fathers tell us that long, long ages past, those three lakes were one large body of water. Where is it now? Have not I seen, in my own lifetime, the last one slowly drying up? Where will our game go when it has quite disappeared? And they laughed at me for telling them. It needs no gift of prophecy to see that. But they heeded me not. What cared they for anything so far in the future as that?

"But," continued the woman, after a pause, dropping her arm in her lap, and speaking in a low, sad voice, "the last time came, and I prophesied, and this time I told wrongly, for Ouiot did not speak through me. We were at war with the southern tribe, and it was revealed to me that our men should conquer. When I told them, a shout went up, and at once they set off for our enemies. It was four days before they came back, but I felt no foreboding, for never before had I been deceived, and why should I be this time? So I waited, confident of the result. Alas! On the fourth day came a messenger with news of the defeat of our army, and the massacre of more than half of the men. For the second time in my life I fainted. When the men returned, they sought me out, and, with cries and curses, drove me from my home, and told me never to come back. But, on account of the position I had held, they gave me this hut by the spring for a dwelling-place, and suffered me to keep you with me. If I had belonged to one of the fierce tribes of Indians to the far east, I think they would have killed me, but we are a milder people. And here we have lived ever since. After a time I was permitted to visit my kindred, but always I am greeted with looks of hatred."

As she crouched in the doorway of the hut, and gazed absently over the distant view, the young woman was thinking of that day when her grandmother had told her past history. Well she remembered that night, and the inspired look on her grandmother's face as she spoke of the future of their people. It was the first time she had ever seen her in that psychic condition, and it was almost terrifying. Since that day, although at rare intervals, her grandmother had given proof of her former power, and in instances touching the welfare of the tribe; but no one save the young woman knew of it.

Then she travelled over in thought the following years, until she became a woman, and was wooed by one of the young men of the tribe, a few months before the date of our story. There had been much opposition to this on the part of her grandmother and of the elders of the tribe; but the young people won the day, and her husband had since made his home with her at the hut. But his marriage with her, in a measure, cut him off from the rest of the tribe; and gradually, as time went on, he had found himself refused the company of his former associates in the hunt, and was forced to make his livelihood, and that of the two women, without the aid of numbers. Until his marriage, the two women had been provided with food by the tribe, but one of the conditions of his wedding the young woman was that all assistance in that line should cease. Henceforward they were to live as though utterly alone. This they had done, and a hard struggle it had been at times, when game was scarce and hard to find. But, though suffering hunger and hardship, they had stayed at the spring, dreading to leave their dwelling-place, and seek other and better hunting-grounds, as is the custom of the Indians when sore pressed for food.

At this particular moment, her husband was absent on one of his hunting trips, which generally kept him away for several days. This time, however, he had been from home longer than usual, and the young wife was looking anxiously for his return, for there was nothing to eat save the remnant of meal in the bottom of the basket, and to-day her grandmother appeared to be worse. The old woman was dying slowly of old age, aided by the peculiar hardship of her long life; she had not left her bed for some time, and the young woman could see that her aged grandparent was not long for this world. During her illness (which, however, was more a gradual breaking down and dying of her strength than actual illness; for her mind seemed to be as clear as ever) she had given evidences of having something in her thought, some instruction or advice she desired to impart to her children, but which, so feeble was she, was beyond her strength to utter. Thus she had lain for three days, motionless, but for the restless turning of the head, and the burning, gleaming eyes seeming to take the place of her voice, and cry out the message her lips refused to speak.

Suddenly the young woman gave a start, and a look of joy passed swiftly across her face, for she saw her husband come around the brow of the hill far below. She rose quickly and hastened to meet him. As she neared him, she saw he was bearing on his back the carcass of a young deer, under the weight of which he staggered up the hill toward her. Running to him she cried:

"Itatli! Oh, you are come in time! You have been away so long! But I see you have had good luck this time in your hunting. How tired and thin you look! Have you been far?" and as she spoke, she took the deer from him, and laid it upon her own strong shoulder.

"Mota, it is a long way I have been, and I am sorely tired. Let me rest and have something to eat, and to-night I will tell you where I have been and what I have seen. How is the grandmother?"

"She is dying, Itatli. She has grown worse every day, and now cannot sit up, and she lies all day so still—all but her eyes. She tries to speak, and I am sure she has something on her mind that she wants to tell us. She will not live long."

Slowly they climbed the hill, with an occasional sentence now and then. Arrived at the hut, the Indian entered, leaned his bow against the wall, near the baskets, and stood regarding the inanimate figure, a sombre expression stealing over his face as he gazed. The woman's eyes were closed, and she seemed to be asleep, nothing but her short, quick breathing showing she was still alive. For some minutes the man stood thus, then turned and strode out of the hut, picking up his bow as he passed it, and carrying it with him. Without a word to his wife, who had begun to cook a piece of the deer meat, and was busily at work over the out-door fire, he occupied himself with his bow and arrows, testing the strength of the cord, made of the intestines of a wild-cat, and examining closely the arrow-heads, tipped with poison, taken from the rattlesnake; but all in an intermittent way, for every few moments he raised his head and gazed long and steadily over the plain to the far distant hills on the southern horizon.

At last his wife called to him that the meal was ready. He went over to the fire and began to eat, while the woman took some of the broth, which she had made out of the meat, put it into a small earthen pot, and carried it to her grandmother, in the hope that she might be able to force a little of it down her throat. It was of no use: the dying woman was insensible to all help from food, and lay as in a stupor, from which it was impossible to rouse her. Mota returned sadly to the fire where her husband was eating as only a hungry man can eat.

They finished their meal in silence, and after the wife had put away the remains of the food, she came over to where her husband was sitting in the opening of the hut, and crouched by his side. There, in the gathering gloom of the night, he told of the experiences of his search for food.

"It was a long, long distance I went, Mota," he began. "I journeyed on and on to the far south, until I reached a river that flows across the plains toward the sea. It was nearing evening of the second day after I came to the river, when suddenly I heard a queer sound as of the steps of a small army of some kind of hard-footed animals. It was far in the distance when first I heard it; for the air was still as though listening to the voice of the Great Spirit, its master; and I listened, rooted to the spot where I stood. What could it be? Never had I heard the tread of so many animals at one time. Nearer they came, and soon I heard the voices of men, speaking to each other, but not in any Indian language I am familiar with, and I know several. But if they were men I must hide, for they would take me prisoner, if they did not kill me, should I be seen. So I ran to the rushes growing on the bank of the river, and sank down among their thickly-growing shoots. The army came nearer steadily, and, in a few moments, I could see them climbing down the steep bank of the river a little way above me. I took one peep, and my breath almost left my body, for what I thought were men before I saw them, now that they came in sight, I knew to be celestial beings."

"But that could not have been, Itatli," exclaimed his wife, "for such a sight would have blinded, if not killed, you."

"I know not about that," answered the man, "but if they were not from above, whence came they? They were like me in shape, stature, and all else but in color and dress. They were white, nearly as white as the snow on the distant mountains, and their bodies were completely covered with their clothes, excepting only their faces and hands. Their clothes were not made of skins, but were something different from anything I had ever seen; it was more like fine basket-work than anything I know of. They had no bows and arrows, such as ours, but straight, long, bright weapons which glittered in the sun. It may have been a strange kind of bow, but I could see no arrows, and they did not shoot with them while near me. On their heads, they wore a large round covering, which shaded them from the hot sun, and on their feet they had queer clothes, shaped like their feet, and these it was which had made me think the sound I heard was that made by animals. But among them were a few who were like us, and they may have been Indians, although they had on clothes like the others; so, perhaps, after all, the white beings were not gods, for the Indians were in their company and lived."

The man had talked in low, earnest tones; but as he advanced in his tale, his voice, though still low, had taken on a penetrating, vibrating quality that thrilled his wife, and reached the ears of the old woman on the couch, seeming to rouse her from her lethargy like a voice from the grave. She had stirred restlessly two or three times, striving ever harder to break the thrall of her weakness: it would have moved the heart of any one beholding her efforts to make herself heard, but she lay unnoticed, for the man was deep in his wonderful narrative, and his wife listening intently, drinking in every word. At last she attracted the attention of the two, for her strenuous efforts to speak resulted in a hoarse, guttural sound deep in her throat. They sprang to their feet, and stepped quickly to the couch. There they saw a surprising change in the countenance of the old woman: her eyes, bright and unclouded as they had been before, now looked at them recognisingly, although they still bore the weighty, thoughtful expression; her mouth, now partly open, was full of resolve, and the lips were just shaping the words she was about to speak, as the two approached:

"Itatli, I heard the words you have spoken this evening, and I, alone, understand them. You know not what manner of men were those you saw; you know not, indeed, whether they be men or angels. I will tell you. They are men like ourselves, but they come from afar. Listen, my children," she continued, her voice growing in power and volume, "I will disclose to you what I have never revealed to any one of our people. About two seasons of rain after I had foretold the future of our tribe, when the last lake should have become entirely dry, I had a revelation of what was to befall all the Indians of this great land, that far surpassed anything I had ever before prophesied. I saw, as in a vision, the great blue sea sparkling in the sun, the little waves rolling softly to the shore, to break into lines of white foam on the sands of the beach at my feet. I was alone, but was not afraid, although I had never before seen the sea, either in my visions or in real life; yet I knew at once what it was. While I gazed at the water, and watched the waves rushing up to my feet, I felt, all at once, as though an unseen power was impelling me to look up. I raised my head and gazed out over the water, and there I saw, far away, a great white object that looked like an immense bird. I knew, as I know all things that occur in my visions, this was a ship.

"Presently, the unseen power, as though whispering in my ear, revealed to me that the ship was full of men from a far country, coming to settle in our land, and that they would subdue the Indians, killing many, taking others captive, and making them work for their masters; and that, later, after many years, the Indians would vanish from the land which had been theirs since the time when Ouiot was on this earth. Then the vision faded slowly from my sight, and I seemed to enter a luminous mist as I felt myself impelled to walk. After what, in my trance, seemed many hours, I came out of the mist on to a level stretch of land, through which flowed a large river. There were mountains on the north, reaching for many miles, and from the west, which was lowland as far as the eye could see, came the cool afternoon sea wind. In the middle of the plain was a great tall house, white with a red roof, and at one end hung some bells in openings made for them in the wall. All around were a great many houses of brush, much like this we are now in, and outside and in were crowds of Indians working like bees, at all kinds of toil, doing many things, too, that we never do, such as planting fields with seeds, and gathering the harvest when it was ripe; making cloth for clothes, such as you, my son, saw those strange men wearing. Then they were making jars and dishes of clay, and weaving baskets, such as we use.

"Suddenly, a little time before sunset, while they were at their busiest, the bells in the big white house began to ring. Every one stopped working and stood facing the building. Then, as the bells were ringing, they bowed their heads. At this moment, I heard, again, the voice which yet was not a voice, revealing to me the meaning of the scene before my eyes. 'Behold,' I seemed to hear, 'the final end of the Indians of this land! See the fate which is awaiting them! All these peoples and tribes, and others far to the north and south of here, will be brought together into places like unto this. They will be made to work at these white men's tasks; give up their own wild, free life in the open country; give up their old customs; give up their own god, even, to pray to the God of their masters. And thus will it be for many years, until the Indians disappear forever; for, after a time, they will grow fewer and fewer until not one shall be left in the whole land which once they owned.' Then what seemed a deep sleep fell upon me, and when I awoke, I was in my own home. I was greatly frightened, but dared not tell any one of my visions; for I knew they would laugh me to scorn, perhaps drive me away, as they did at the last."

As the old woman described this picture of the future revealed to her, her agitation increased. She raised herself on an arm, and with the other stretched out, she swept her hand along the horizon, from the south to the north, saying, as she did so:

"This is the land of the Indians; this Ouiot gave to our fathers, and they gave it to us. While the sun has been travelling over his path in the sky for many hundred years, we, and our fathers before us, for generations, have lived in this land. But now the end is come. We must give way before a people stronger than we; give up our land to them and vanish."

Her voice increased in volume as she spoke, until, at the close, it was as powerful as in former days. When she had ceased speaking, she paused, with arm still outstretched, as though transfixed. She gazed steadily across the level plain to the distant mountains, motionless and rigid, while the two young Indians waited, awed and afraid, minute after minute, for they knew not what.

After a long silence, the aged sibyl let fall her arm, and dropped back suddenly on to the couch. The fire of prophecy in her eyes was still undimmed; but turning toward the two waiting ones, she spoke again, yet as if coming back to the present:

"Mota, Itatli, I am going to the distant home of our

people, where all are happy. It will be but a few hours before I shall leave you. Do you, my son, after I am dead, go to the village, and tell the chief men all that I have revealed to you to-night. Tell them that, with my last breath, I spoke the truth revealed to me by the gods above. Tell them that the only safety for them, and their children after them, is to live with the strange white men who are come to our land; that they must be at peace with the strangers, live with them, and do all that is commanded them; that this is the only way they can put off the evil day when they shall disappear forever. And it is for a time only at best; but it is better to do that than to resist them, for they are too strong to be driven back. But I fear they will not listen to my words which you shall speak. And if so, you, my children, must leave here and go to the south, through the pass in the mountains, then toward the setting sun until you come to the river; and there you will find the strange men, as in my vision. Put yourselves under their care, and perhaps Ouiot will spare you, and the others there before you, from the fate of the rest of the tribes in this land."

Her voice sank to a whisper, so that it was with difficulty they made out her last words. Closing her eyes, she lay gasping for some minutes; after this, she fell into a comatose state, from which she did not revive again. Hour after hour passed, the two watchers crouching motionless, without a word, regarding the fleeting breath of the dying woman. Shortly before the dawn began to lighten the horizon, a tremor passed through the body of the sufferer; a long, feeble sigh issued from her lips, and the aged, distrusted seer was no more.

The young woman, on seeing this, broke out into bitter wailing, swaying slowly forward and backward, while her husband sat with his head bowed on his knees. Their first thought was of utter bereavement, for to these two lonely ones, and especially to the woman, the grandparent had been not only the sole member of their tribe they had known for years, but she had proved to them a help, at times through her singular gift. On several occasions, in seasons of little game, had she told the man in which direction to go for the best results. Once, at her instance, they had migrated to a distant spring she had known in her youth, where the three were safe from the murderous designs of the warlike tribe coming to their country from the north.

Finally the man bethought himself of the last behest of the dead woman. "I go to the village, Mota," he said hoarsely, and without another word left the hut and set off down the hill.

The woman moved not, but remained as before, near the bed of her grandmother. There she sat, on the earthen floor, without taking her eyes from the face of the dead, until her husband returned, nearly three hours later.

"It was no use," he exclaimed sadly, "they would not listen, but told me to go back and bury the grandmother; they would not come with me."

Mota replied not.

That night, as the sun was setting, the two lone creatures made a grave on the hill a few feet from the hut, and there they buried the mortal remains of the old Indian woman. It was a sad, silent rite; both felt deeply the absence of all their friends and kindred; the lack of all the customary wailing proper to the solemn service of burial; but, above all, the want of belief in the dead woman's prophecy. That gave the poignant touch to their sorrow. Sadly and silently, as they had buried the dead, they returned to their hut in the gathering shades of night.

The next morning, these two bereaved ones, packing up their few simple belongings, stole sorrowfully away from their home. They knew not what was before them, scarcely anything of the country whither they were bound; but such was their faith in the dead woman's word, that they did not falter in their resolution to fulfill her admonition.

The hut, and all belonging to it, is long passed away; and the spring, also, has disappeared, drying up till merely a stony furrow in the ground shows where it once had its course. Only the lonely grave on the hillside remains to mark the ancient Indian habitation here, and that, to-day, is almost obliterated. As for the village beyond in the cañon, that, too, is no more; hardly a vestige can now be found to tell us that here, long ago, was a thriving Indian settlement. All is silent and deserted. Truly, as the aged Indian prophetess foretold, has the aborigine vanished from the land.

THE FLIGHT OF PADRE PEYRI

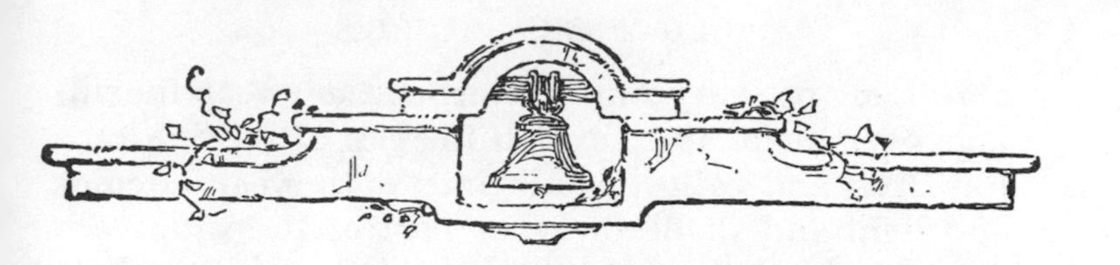

THE FLIGHT OF PADRE PEYRI

ONE of the few settlements of the old mission Indians remaining in California is Pala, a little village tucked away amidst some of the most charming scenery to be found in the southern part of the state. It is twenty miles east from Mission San Luis Rey, of which mission it was an *asistencia*, or branch, and twenty-four miles from Oceanside, the nearest point on the coast. The village stands in a valley which is completely surrounded by mountains, high and low, far and near, uniting with it in a succession of beautiful pictures around the entire horizon. To the east, the mountains pile themselves up into huge masses, their tips hidden frequently by clouds, and by the fogs of early morning; toward the west, they fall away into low-lying hills, allowing the sea-breeze of every warm afternoon to sweep the village over them, and through the gap of the San Luis Rey River and Valley. At all times of the year the color and light and shade in every part of the valley are most lovely, delighting the artist's eye with a whole gamut of aërial perspective; but it is in the spring that the hillsides and valley put on their most gorgeous robes, from the lightest tints of yellow and green, down through every hue and tone of red, blue and purple, soft and brilliant, pricked out here and there with spots of intense, flaming yellow and orange, or deepest crimson. Such color scenes are not common even in California; but on account of its comparative inaccessibility, few people visit Pala, and the village has been left much to itself in these latter days of American life in the state. The Indians live the life of the poorest class of Mexicans, dwell in adobe huts, and pursue an agricultural occupation.

During the last week of May, 1895, I passed two days in this interesting place, exploring the remains of the *asistencia,* and sketching the unique bell-tower and near-by mission houses. I was an object of interest to all who saw me, but was not favored with much company until the second afternoon, when, after I had passed an hour or so in the *campo santo,* an old Indian slowly appeared and greeted me. He must have been nearly eighty years old, and he was obliged to use a cane to assist his slow and faltering steps. Several times during the two days I had seen him, sitting in the sun on the rough porch of a house close by, or ambling slowly about, and had been struck with his appearance. Although bent with his years, he was tall, and, in his younger days, must have had a graceful, as well as powerful, figure, traces of it remaining still, in spite of his decrepitude. But his face was the most noticeable thing about him. Notwithstanding the dimness of age, there was a wonderful amount of intelligence and animation in his expression, and the deep, black eyes could hardly have been brighter and more piercing at the age of forty than they now appeared. His long straight hair was still thick, but very grey. He wore the ordinary dress of the poor man. He was, in fine, a specimen of what the missions could do with the Indians when working on the best material to be found among them.

"Buenos dias, Señor," he said gravely, as he came near.

"Buenos dias."

"Will the Señor be disturbed if I stay here awhile and watch him work?" he continued in Spanish, which he spoke rather slowly, but with as much ease and correctness as a Mexican.

I answered I should be glad to have him remain so long as he pleased, and, in return, after he had seated himself beside me on an old ruined adobe wall, asked if he had lived long here.

"For over sixty years, Señor."

"And where did you spend your early years, for I think you have seen many more than sixty?" I asked.

"Si, Señor, I am eighty-one now. Until I was about twenty, I lived at Mission San Luis Rey, twenty miles

from here. Has the Señor ever seen San Luis Rey?"

I nodded, continuing with my sketch.

"Ah! that was a beautiful mission sixty years ago," the old man said, in a tone of sad retrospect.

"Tell me about it," I said. "In those days, sixty years ago, the mission must have been perfect, with no ruins to mar its beauty. And were there not many neophytes at that time?" I added.

"Señor, San Luis Rey was the largest mission in California. So much larger than this place, although Pala had many more Indians in those days, before the padres were driven away, that it seemed to me like a city. There were more than two thousand Indians, and all worked busily from morning until night, the men plowing and planting in the fields, or making adobes for building houses, and the women weaving and sewing and cooking. Every one had something to do, and knew it must be done, and all were willing and glad to do it; for we all dearly loved the padre, he was so good, and it was a happiness to do what he demanded of us."

"You speak of Padre Peyri, do you not?" I asked.

"*Si,* Señor. Padre Peyri was the head of the mission, and no one could do anything unless he had the padre's consent. There was almost always a second padre there, but this second padre never stayed long, and when one went away, another would come in his place; but Padre Peyri was there all the time, and never left the mission until he went back to Mexico."

"And what," I asked, "did you do in those days,

before you were large enough for a man's work?"

"I worked with the children, for the children had their own work to do just the same as the grown people. We had to go to school at the mission every day, to learn to speak Spanish, and to say the *doctrina cristiana,* to read and write; but not all the children could get so far as to write, for it was hard for them to learn, and only the brightest ones were ever able to write more than their names. But it was not so hard for me, for I wished to learn, and the padres liked to teach me. Then, after school, we had other work—to fetch wood for the fires; to drive the cows to the fields; to feed and water the horses at the mission, and all such things that boys can do. There were a hundred boys or more in the country around, and many of them seldom came to the mission except for school and Sunday mass; but there were always enough, and more than enough, to do all the work, and they had plenty of time for play. But my work was different from that of the other boys. I was one of the two boys who waited on the padres at meal times, swept the mission rooms and walks, and were ready to do any errands the padres wished. Then, for three years, I was one of the altar boys, until I could play well enough to go into the choir. And that is what I liked better than anything else—to play on my violin. I began to learn when I was twelve years old. I used to listen to the boys of the choir, when they were practising their mass music, and again on Sundays in the church, and wish I, too, could learn to make that beautiful music. Many times I implored the padre to let me learn, and he would say: 'After a little, my son, when you are old enough; it is a difficult instrument to learn.' I knew he was right, but did not like to wait. At last, however, he told me I was to begin, and the very next day gave me a violin, and sent me to the choir teacher. It was a happy day for me."

"Tell me something about Padre Peyri," I asked.

"Señor, I could talk all day long about that good man. He was so kind and gentle to all, that no one but would have been willing to die for him, if he had asked such a thing. He was not a large man, but was as strong as many of the Indians, and he worked as hard as any one of us. I have heard my mother tell how he helped with his own hands to build the church and the other houses of the mission, and worked all day, so long as it was light, hardly stopping to take time to eat. She said he seemed to think of nothing but to get all the buildings finished, and was unhappy until that was done. She saw him on the day he first came from Mission San Diego with a few workmen and soldiers to start the mission. It was in the afternoon, and the padre and his men passed the time till nightfall in making a few huts for themselves like those of the Indians. The next morning, before he would permit anything else to be done, he made an altar of earth, which he covered all over with the green growing grass, and there offered up a sacrifice to his God. He had with him some children he had brought from San Diego, and after the mass he baptised them. My mother and some of the Indians had been to San

Diego, to the mission there, and were not afraid, but nearly all the Indians did not dare come near.

"As soon as the mass was ended, the padre marked out on the ground the lines for the mission buildings, and the men went to work making adobes. After a few days, the Indians began to lose their fear of the *cristianos,* and it was not long before they were helping in all the work to be done. The padre payed them every day for what they did; he would give them clothes or something to eat, and they were very glad to work for him; and it was only a short time when a great crowd was busy on the buildings. My mother told me all this, Señor, for that was long before I was born,—more than fifteen years. She was a young girl then. My mother told the Indians how good the padres were to them at San Diego, and did all she could to bring them to work for the mission. I was her first child, and, at her wish, the padre named me after himself—Antonio. But all the mission buildings were finished in a few years, and they have never been changed except by falling into ruins. I have not been to San Luis Rey for a long, long time, for I cannot bear to go there and see the poor old buildings tumbling to the ground—at least that is what they were doing until Padre O'Keefe came from Santa Bárbara to live there and take charge of the mission. I am glad it is in his care; but he cannot bring back the old days, for the Indians are nearly all gone now.

"But the Señor wishes to hear about the padre. I think Padre Peyri was nearly fifty years old when I was born, and he had been at the mission all the time since he started it, about fifteen years before. How he did love his mission, and how proud he was of it! And he was right to be proud, for it was the finest mission in the country, and the largest also. Every one who came there praised the padre for the wonders he had done; and that made him very happy. After his day's work was over, he liked to walk about in the neighborhood, looking at, and seeing, everything—the ground, the trees and the sky, listening to the singing of the birds, and watching the sun sink out of sight in the west; but above all else, gazing at the mission, at the beautiful big church, and the building and arches around the patio. Sometimes when I came to him at his bidding, I would see him smiling to himself, as though he was happy to have been able to raise up such a good work to his Lord.

"But alas! Señor, those happy times could not last always. I do not understand very well the trouble that was between the missions and the Governor—it has always been too much for my poor head—but I suppose the Señor knows all about it. The Governor wished the Indians to be taken away from the missions, and live in *pueblos* of their own; but the Indians did not like it, nor the padres either; and it made trouble for many years. I was too young to think much about it, but I used to hear the Indians talking among themselves of what they heard from time to time. I asked my father why the Governor could take the Indians away from the missions. He told me it was the wish of Mexico that we should not live in the missions any longer, but have our own land, and work for money. 'But must we leave our padre here, and not see him any more?' I asked my father.

"'We may have to go away from here,' he answered, 'but the padre would be our padre still, and we should see him at mass and at other times; but it would not be as it is now.'

"'I will never leave here,' I said to him, 'as long as the padre stays; I do not want to go off to work for myself.'

"But the change, Señor, was long in coming, and before it did come, there was another and a greater change at the mission. Well do I remember the day when first I knew, without a doubt, that our old life was at an end. It was a dark and stormy Saturday in early winter. Just before nightfall, a traveller arrived at the mission from the north. Alone and riding slowly a tired horse, which looked as if it had been driven long and hard, he approached, gazing around at the church and all the buildings within sight. I was driving one of the cows home from the pasture to provide milk for the padre's supper, and saw him as he reached the mission. As soon as I came up to him, he asked me:

"'Is the padre here?'

"'*Si,* Señor.'

"'Tell him Don Manuel wishes to see him at once,' he said, in a commanding tone.

"Calling one of the boys not far away to look after the cow, and to take care of the stranger's horse, I went to the padre's room and knocked. After waiting a moment, and getting no reply, I knocked again. Hearing no sound, I opened the door and went in. The room was empty, but the door leading into a small side room, from which was an entrance into the church for the padre's use, stood open, and I knew he was in the church. At any other time I would have hesitated, but the traveller had spoken so sternly that I dared not delay, so went on into the church. There was the padre kneeling before the altar of our patron saint, San Luis Rey, his rosary of beautiful gold beads and ivory cross in his hands; but so still one would have said he himself was a statue. I waited again, in hopes he would finish his prayer and come away; but the minutes went by and still he did not move. At last I stepped toward him, stumbling a little against one of the seats that he might know some one was there. He heard the sound and, rising slowly, turned and came toward the door near which I stood. When he saw me he asked what was wanted. I told him.

"'Is it come at last?' he said, more to himself than to me, and walked slowly, with bowed head, out of the church. I followed, closing the door of the church and of the little side room, and saw once more the traveller, as he rose from his knees, after receiving the padre's blessing. A moment later he followed the padre into his room.

"I did not see them again until supper time, when I had to wait at table. They had been some minutes at supper, but were so occupied with their talk that they had eaten scarcely anything. The stranger was speaking when I went in.

"'But, padre,' he said, 'what will become of your charge here, if you carry out your intention? You know they look up to you as the head and soul of this great mission, and would be, indeed, as sheep without their shepherd, if you—'

"'My son,' interrupted the padre, with a look toward me, 'we will speak of that another time.'

"Nothing more was said until after I had left them. I had seen the look the padre sent in my direction. Had not it been at a time when every one was fearing a change of some kind at the mission, I should have thought nothing of it; but at the time, I knew we might expect something to occur almost any day; so that when he interrupted the stranger, it was only after enough had been said to fill me with fear. I knew, from what he said about the sheep being without a shepherd, that we might, in some way, lose our padre. As soon as I was free I hastened out to find Miguel, the boy who had taken the stranger's horse. He had gone to his house, a little way from the church.

"'Miguel,' I asked, 'do you know who is this visitor, Don Manuel, and why he is come?'

"'He came from Los Angeles, on important business with the padre,' Miguel replied.

"'How do you know he is from Los Angeles, and that his business is important?'

"'Because, while you were seeking the padre, Don Manuel was so impatient at your delay that he could not stand still, and kept striding up and down the length of the arcade, muttering to himself. Once I caught the words that if the padre but knew the importance of his business, he would make great haste. When I led away his horse, he told me to take good care of it, for it must carry him as far on his way tomorrow as it had to-day from Los Angeles.'

"'And what is this important business?'

"'*Quien sabe!*' answered Miguel, with a shrug of his shoulders.

"This was very little to be sure, and it served only to increase my fear that all was not right.

"But I heard nothing further that night.

"The next day was the Sabbath. Nothing occurred before mass; breakfast was eaten by the stranger alone in the padres' dining-room, and the padre was not seen by any one until the hour for mass. The other padre was here at Pala to take the place of the *fraile* who was sick. The beautiful church was crowded, every neophyte casting a glance now and then at Don Manuel, who was seated in front, watching the door by which the padre was to enter. But it was not until all had begun to wonder what was the reason for his delay, and to grow uneasy and whisper softly to each other, looking at the stranger as though they connected him with some trouble about to befall the mission and their padre. For in those days very little was necessary to stir up fears of a change all knew might come suddenly at any time. At last the door opened, and the padre came slowly into the church. He was pale, and looked sad and troubled, but went through the service in his usual manner. But when he came to the sermon, it seemed as if he could not go on. He did not take a text from which to preach, but began at once to talk to us in his earnest, gentle voice, saying we must look to God as our father, as one who loved us and would guide us in all this life. Padre Peyri did not preach to us like the fathers at other missions: he seldom said anything about hell and the punishments waiting for us if we were wicked, but talked to us and preached about the love of God and His Son Jesus Christ, and our duty to them, not from fear of future punishment, but because we owed it to them, as we owed our earthly parents love and respect. This morning he was more than ever solemn, and before the close of his short talk, many of his listeners had tears in their eyes. More than once he had to stop for a moment, to regain control of his voice which, all through his talk, trembled and sometimes was hardly above a whisper. As soon as the service was ended, he left the church, followed quickly by the stranger.

"I hastened from the choir and church to the padre's room to be ready at hand in case he should want anything. He was not there, but I found him in the patio, talking earnestly with Don Manuel, as they walked up and down the cloister. As soon as he saw me, he told me to give orders to have the visitor's horse ready for him immediately after dinner. I did so, and on coming back from the large dining-room, where I told my errand to one of the *mozos*, found the padre and Don Manuel just sitting down to their own dinner. The padre ate little; but there was nothing else to make me think that anything was wrong, and had not it been for the night before, and the morning's mass, I should have thought nothing of it. But now every little thing was large and important in my eyes; and although nothing was said but what might have been said by any visitor at any time, I grew more and more heavy-hearted. After they had finished eating, which they did very quickly, the stranger prepared to leave. Gathering up his *sombrero* and *zarape,* and receiving a small package, which looked like a bundle of letters, from the padre, he strode out to his horse, already waiting for him in front of the building, the padre close behind him.

"I took my place by the horse, and pretended to be looking at the saddle, to see that everything was right, while I tried to hear what the padre and Don Manuel were saying; but they spoke too low for me to make out more than a word now and then. I heard Don Manuel say 'San Diego;' 'the Pocahontas, a small ship but;' 'Spain,' and a few other words of no significance. Padre Peyri said hardly a word, but stood with bowed head, and eyes cast on the ground. At last Don Manuel knelt to receive the padre's blessing, and with a last low sentence, and an '*adios,*' spoken aloud, as he sprang to his horse, he dashed off down the hill until he came to the mission road which runs from San Diego into the far north. The padre watched him turn his horse's head toward the south, and disappear behind a hill; a few minutes later he came into sight again as he ascended another hill until at last he stood on the top. With a long look at the rider hurrying away in the distance, the padre turned and, without a word to me, went into the house and shut himself in his room.

"Señor, that was the last time I saw him at the mission. Padre Ánzar, who had been at Pala that day, returned to the mission in the afternoon, and I saw him at supper, but Padre Peyri did not come out of his room the rest of the day. Late that night I wandered around the church, so sad and full of fear of what I knew was coming, that I could not sleep. There was a light in the church, and I was sure the padre was in there, but, of course, I could not go in to see, and speak to him. After a little while the light disappeared, and I went back to my bed.

"Although I now felt certain I knew what the padre was going to do, from what I had heard and seen, yet I knew nothing of the time, and did not dream it was so near. But early the next morning I knew all. I was on my way to the padre's house, when I met Miguel coming toward me on the run. As soon as he came near he cried to me:

"'Antonio, *el padre se ha ido* (the padre is gone)! His horse is not here, nor his saddle.'

"My heart stood still. So all that I had feared the day before was come true, and our beloved padre had left us. But how suddenly it had taken place! I thought of 'San Diego' and 'the small ship Pocahontas,' and knew all. I had not seen Miguel since my talk with him two nights before, and he knew nothing of what had occurred. I now told him everything.

"'*Dios mio!* Our padre gone away, not to come back? Oh, why did he go? Why did not he stay with us? What shall we do without him?' he exclaimed.

"While Miguel was crying in this manner, I was like one stunned, and knew not what to do. Suddenly a thought came to me.

"'Miguel, let us follow him, and, if we can, persuade him to come back. I know he did not go willingly, but was driven to it by the Governor and his people; for you know he has often said that here was his home, and here he intended to stay until his death.'

"'But, Antonio, what can we two do? He would not listen to us, and, besides, he must be too far ahead now to be overtaken. And the ship may have left before we get to San Diego. You did not hear when it was to sail?'

"'No, but we can come up with him, I am sure, before he reaches San Diego, if we waste no time. Come, I am going to tell my father, and get my horse, and be off.' And I started on the run for my father's house, which was not far from the church. I found him just leaving for his work, and told him, in a few words, what had happened. He was not so surprised as I thought he would be, for he was an old man, and knew more of all that was taking place in the country, than was possible for me, a mere boy.

"'Go, Antonio,' he said. 'I shall follow you;' and he turned away into the house.

"I waited not to see what he would do, but darted away, and, catching my horse, was off as hard as I could ride. Before I had gone many rods, I heard a horse's gallop behind me, and, looking back, saw Miguel at full speed. I stopped to permit him to come up with me, and then, without a word, we went on together.

"There are nearly ten leagues between San Luis Rey and San Diego, Señor; and as we were determined to reach there by noon, we said very little during the whole ride, but urged our horses to their utmost. After going a few miles, we came to the shore, and went along by the ocean, sometimes on the beach itself, sometimes on the *mesa* above. But swiftly as we went, the sun was still quicker, and it was nearly noon when we came in sight of San Diego. We hastened on, past houses, the presidio, and down to the edge of the water, taking no notice of the men, women and children, who gazed wonderingly after us. Out in the bay, not far from the shore, lay a ship with sails spread, ready to start with the first puff of wind, which began faintly to blow as we reached the water. On the deck there were many people, passengers and sailors, and among them we saw our padre, a little apart from the others, and gazing toward the land he was leaving. By his side stood Don Manuel, who had been at the mission the day before, and with them were two of the mission Indians. I envied them, Señor, and wished I could have been there also, for my heart was breaking at the thought of losing my beloved padre. At first he did not notice us, but when, with a cry, we called to him, he started as he saw us standing on the beach, with our arms held out to him. Just at that instant, we heard a distant sound of horses coming hard and fast over the ground toward us. Looking around, we saw a sight that made us thrill: a great throng of men, each one urging on with whip and spur the horse he was riding. We did not at once know what it meant, but, in a second or two, understood. It was a band of Indians from our mission. Madly they dashed down to the shore, sprang from their horses, and fell on their knees—some on the beach, some half in the water, so great was the crowd—imploring, with heart-breaking cries, our padre to have pity on them and not leave them. There were nearly five hundred men, and their lamentations were terrible to hear.

"But the sails had filled with the freshening breeze, and the ship was fast getting under way. The padre gazed at us all, long and sorrowfully, and, with arms raised up to Heaven, in a faltering voice, which we could scarcely hear from the increasing distance, called down the blessing of God on us. With groans and cries we watched the ship sail away, and as it faded into the distance, we saw our beloved padre kneeling on the deck in prayer.

"Señor, there is no more to tell. We waited there on the beach until the ship had disappeared; then slowly, one by one, found each our horse, and set out for the mission. All night we rode, not caring how or when we should get there. When we reached the mission, we found the women and children gathered together, waiting for us. As soon as they saw us they burst out weeping and lamenting, for, by our manner, they knew our padre was gone. Silently we turned loose our horses, and went back to our old life and work, but with sorrow in our hearts. That is all, Señor."

I had listened to the old man with great and constantly increasing interest, and long before he had finished, found myself with brush held idly in my hand. He had told his story with simple earnestness, crossed, now and then, with deep emotion, as his love for the Franciscan father, and sorrow at his loss, came to the surface. After an interval of silence, I asked him if he had ever heard of the padre since that day.

"Only two or three times," he answered. "A few months afterward we had news of him from Mexico; he was then about to return to Spain. Two years after we heard he was at his old home and, a little later, that he was gone to Rome. Some one told us he lived there till his death, but we never knew positively.

Padre Peyri is one of the most picturesque figures in California's mission history: the zeal he showed in calling his mission into existence; the intensity of enthusiasm with which he labored for it; his long career of usefulness; the love the neophytes had for him; his agony at the ruthless destruction of the missions—too great for him to endure, old and feeble as he then was growing; and his dramatic departure, hastening away under cover of the night, to escape the importunities of his devoted flock: all this had been pictured with keen clearness in the old Indian's simple tale.

I thanked him for his story as he rose to go. Wishing me "adios" with grave politeness, he walked slowly away, and left me to dream of the old mission times, full of color and romance, which have given so much to the present day, until the sun sinking behind the hills in the west recalled me to myself and my surroundings.

I fear I shall never again see Pala; but I shall not forget its charm and beauty, the quaint old *campanario* and near-by buildings, and, above all, Antonio, the Indian, and his tale of mission life in the old days.

FATHER ZALVIDEA'S MONEY

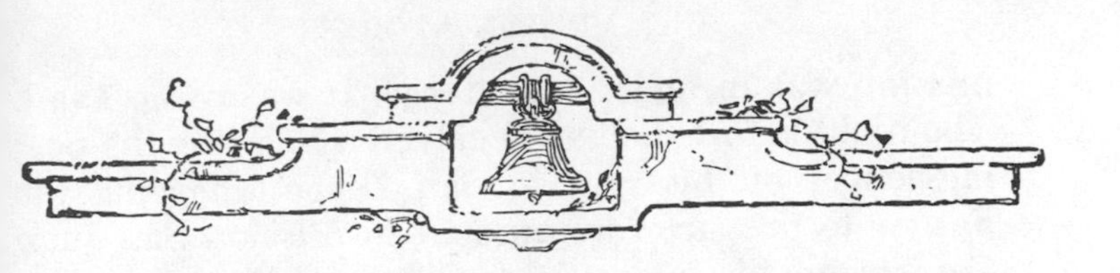

FATHER ZALVIDEA'S MONEY

FATHER ZALVIDEA was in despair! After having lived for twenty years at Mission San Gabriel, devoting himself all that time to bringing the mission to a condition of so great size and wealth that it took its place at the head of nearly all of the missions of Nueva California, toiling from morning until night with untutored neophytes and striving to hammer something of civilisation into their heads—now he was to be removed. He had seen this very thing threatening for many days, but had hoped and prayed that it might not be; he had mustered up boldness enough to address President Tapis at Monterey, beseeching that he might be continued at San Gabriel, bringing to bear the weight of all he had done, and the flourishing condition the mission was in under his charge. It was of no avail. The night before, he had received a letter by the post messenger on his way to San Diego, charging the Father to prepare for removal to Mission San Juan Capistrano, his future field of work. After a sleepless night of vain repining, he had risen early and wandered out into his garden, back of the church, his favorite resort when in a meditative mood, or when he wished to escape intrusion of whatever sort.

Father Zalvidea's garden was a warm, sunny place, filled to overflowing with flowers and plants and trees. It covered nearly an acre of ground, bounded on one side by the church, on part of the adjoining side by the Father's house, close by the church; from here the ground sloped gradually to the west, leaving open to view the San Gabriel Mountains, towering high above the plain. The Father had planned this garden soon after coming to the mission, and had laid it out with all the talent of a landscape artist. In the corner bounded by the church and his house, he had planted most of the trees—olive, lemon and peach, and a few palms—disposing them skillfully for shade, while at the same time leaving vistas of the adobe church, golden yellow in the sunlight; beyond were placed the flowering plants—roses in immense numbers, a great variety of lilies of different tints, a few century plants, one of them with its huge flower stalk high in air, and a large passion vine, trained along the adobe wall enclosing the garden on the west. These were the most prominent of the plants, brought from Mexico and Spain, reminding him of his old home; and interspersed with these were a goodly number of vegetables, for this garden was not wholly for pleasure, but served as a source of supply for the Father's table. Paths there were none. Every spot of ground, where there was nothing growing, was hard and smooth like a path, baked as it was by the sun after every rain. At first the Father had tried to grow grass in some parts of his garden, but soon gave it up on account of the constant attention it needed, and disliking the tough wiry grass, native to the region, he trained his plants to cover the ground, letting them spread and wander much at their will. Here was his rest from the many and varied labors in a Nueva California mission; and here he was to be found when at leisure, seeing if his plants were given the proper attention by his gardener, studying changes from time to time in their arrangement, or wandering about, now here, now there, with eyes bent on the ground, meditating on his duties, or gazing off to the distant horizon, and dreaming of his early life in his boyhood home.

But this morning Father Zalvidea was thinking of anything but Spain, or even of his garden, as he passed slowly back and forth among the plants. His thoughts were occupied with the instructions he had received the night before. One must put one's self in the Father's place, and know something of his life and surroundings, to appreciate the reason for his dislike to the proposed change. The missions in Nueva California were lonely, isolated spots of civilisation in the midst of many Indian tribes. Each one, twenty to fifty miles distant from the neighboring mission on either side, lived, in a great measure, solely for itself, as it was dependent, in most things, on itself alone. There was communication, of course, between the different missions, with the president at Monterey, and with Mexico; but, occasionally, weeks would go by without a single messenger from the outside world, during which time each mission was a little world by itself. This tended to strengthen the love for locality, which was still farther increased from the fathers' having no family ties, leading them, each one, in his celibate state, to become more deeply attached to his own particular field of labor, with an intensity not often seen in other classes of men. Thus our Father Zalvidea had been so long at Mission San Gabriel, that he had come to look on it almost as his own, in more senses than the one strictly of being its religious and temporal head. He had carried on the good work, begun by his predecessor, Father Sanchez, and had brought the mission to such a state of prosperity, that it was second to none in wealth, and to but few in number of Indian neophytes. Now, as he wandered around in his garden, he gazed at the buildings of his establishment scattered, near and far, in every direction; at the church, close by, which, although not as fine as those at some of the missions —San Luis Rey and Santa Bárbara, for instance— was a good solid structure, imposing in its appearance of strength; his own abode adjoining; the low adobe houses of the Indians everywhere; the corrals of livestock on the foot-hills in the distance. Finally his eye rested on the vineyards stretching away toward the north and west, so far that they seemed without end. These vineyards were the pride of the Father's heart, for the culture of the grape was one of his hobbies, and here at San Gabriel he had carried out his theories in viticulture so successfully that his vineyards, and the wine and brandy made from them, were famous throughout the length of the land, and much sought after by the other missions, as well as by Mexico. No wonder the Father was proud of his success, for this product was a mine of wealth to the mission. Now, however, there was no pride in his glance, as he looked long and sorrowfully at his vineyards; he was thinking gloomily that they were no longer his, and that he must leave this place, which he was come to love with all the repressed passion of his heart. It was not as though he were going to a poor and mean mission, as were some of those in Nueva California. Father Zalvidea had been more than once to San Juan Capistrano, fifty miles south of San Gabriel, and knew well that it was large, although not as rich as it had been at one time; but his was the nature of the cat, which always returns to its old home. Father Zalvidea knew a priest was needed at San Juan Capistrano, and none was as available as himself; but he was human, and this last sacrifice of self was more than he could make without a murmur.

At last he returned to his house, and, after breakfast, began to make his preparations. A week later saw him leaving the mission with his personal belongings, the most valuable of which appeared to be a heavy wooden box, about the size and shape of a brick, and which he would not allow out of his own hands, but carried with him, fastened to the pommel of his saddle. What was in this box no one knew but the Father himself.

Behold Father Zalvidea at Mission San Juan Capistrano! Although at first murmuring at the change of his scene of labor, yet, after finding it inevitable, he had submitted to it with all due humility, and with energy and even enthusiasm had thrown himself into the work at hand. Mission San Juan Capistrano was fallen away sadly from the high position it had held ten years before: neophytes were still many, but they had been allowed to follow their own devices; the religious life, consequently, was neglected, as well as the cultivation of the mission lands. It was a sad prospect that met the Father's eyes, the first time he took a survey of the fields and corrals and vineyards of the mission. On every side his well-trained eye saw the marks of lack of care in husbandry—the fields of wheat and corn were only half cultivated; the livestock in the corrals looked poor and thin; while as for the vineyards—! Father Zalvidea sighed deeply as he gazed at what were the merest apology for vineyards, judging from his high standard, and compared them mentally with those cared for so lovingly at Mission San Gabriel. He saw, at a glance, just what was needed, and set about bringing them up to a point somewhat approaching his ideal.

But before giving his attention to these mundane things, Father Zalvidea had to do much for the spiritual side of the mission and its people; for it was in a more deplorable state in this respect than in that of material welfare. Fourteen years before, Mission San Juan Capistrano had had the finest church in Nueva California, the pride of the whole country. Father Zalvidea had been present at its dedication, the occasion of great ceremony amidst a vast throng of neophytes, and all the Spanish dignitaries that could be gathered together. But the mission had enjoyed its beautiful church only a few years when it suffered a most awful calamity. One Sunday morning, when the church was crowded with Indians at mass, there was heard in the hush of prayer, a distant noise, like the sound of a great rush of stormwind, which, a moment later, reached the mission, and with the rocking of the earth and the rending of walls, the tower of the new church fell on the people below, shrieking as they fled. Forty were killed on the spot, as well as many wounded. This catastrophe was by far the worst ever visited on the missions, and it was long before San Juan Capistrano recovered from the blow—never, in fact, so far as the church was concerned, for it was too badly injured to be repaired, and the fathers could not summon up energy enough to build another. Since that dire Sabbath, a room in the adjoining building had been used as a church. Father Zalvidea's greatest desire, next to seeing the vineyards brought up to their proper condition, was to build a new church, and these were the only mitigating circumstances in his regretted change of residence; but he had been only a few days at his new home, when he gave up his purpose with regard to the church; it was beyond his power, as he saw. San Juan Capistrano had been too long on the decline, and the neophytes were too indifferent, to undertake this work.

So our Father Zalvidea confined himself to the simple religious duties of his position, and left such grand projects as building a new church to the future. He had enough, and more than enough, to occupy all his time, and he soon ceased to sigh for his old home at San Gabriel, indeed, almost to think of it. It was only at rare intervals that he found time, after the day's work was done, to take a little *pasear* in the mission garden in front of the monastery. But this garden was a poor makeshift; the plants were of the commonest kinds, and were choked with weeds. Still, the Father found comfort in it, and with his oversight it was soon a fairly respectable garden. So the months flew by.

It was more than a year after Father Zalvidea's advent at Mission San Juan Capistrano, when he bethought himself one day of the little wooden box he had brought with him. On arriving, he had deposited it temporarily at the bottom of a large chest which stood in his room, and which was used for storing away papers and records of the mission. Hidden as the box was, under piles of papers, the Father felt tolerably safe regarding his treasure, and immured as he had been ever since, in the busy affairs needing his whole time and attention, he had almost forgotten it. But on this day he had made up his mind to hide it more effectually. Late that night, after the entire mission was still in sleep, he took out the box, placed it on the table, and by the light of a candle, opened it with a small key which he wore, hung by a slender black silk cord, round his neck underneath his Franciscan robe. Inside were five gleaming rows of gold coins—bright new Spanish *onzas,* every one looking as if just fresh from the mint. There were one hundred and twenty-five coins, each worth about sixteen dollars of American money, making the contents of the box amount to two thousand dollars—a goodly sum, indeed, for a poor Spanish priest in Nueva California to possess. Lying on top of the rows of coins was a slip of paper, on which was written in Spanish:

"My dearest one, pray to God and Our Lady to bless your poor Dolores."

Father Zalvidea read the paper, then kissing it passionately, fell on his knees, and, with trembling voice, offered up his petitions to Christ for a blessing on the loved one in the far away land.

This box contained the romance of Father Zalvidea's life. Years before, when a young man, and ere he had had any thought of becoming a priest, he had been enamoured of a beautiful Andalucian maiden, who returned his love. But Dolores's father was rich, and looked with disfavor upon poor José Zalvidea, and at length forced his daughter to marry a suitor he had chosen for her—a man three times her age, but with a fortune equal to that which was to be hers at her father's death; for she was his only child. José, heart-broken, entered a seminary to study for the priesthood, and gave himself up to his new work, striving to drown his sorrow. A few years later, he was selected to make one of a number of young priests to go to Mexico. The last time he had heard confessions in the parish church, a woman, heavily veiled, entered the confessional, and, in a whisper, interrupted by sobs, asked for his blessing. At her first word he recognized Dolores's voice, and with a smothered cry, fell back, almost unconscious, in his seat. This was the first time he had seen her since her unhappy marriage, five years before. Recovering himself, he asked her, coldly, why she was there. With sobs she told him she had a small box which she would leave in the confessional for him. On his asking what was in it, and what she wished him to do with it, she said it was a small sum of money which he must take with him on his journey, and always keep by him, and if, at any time, or when old age overtook him, he were in want, to use it. "You are going far away," she said. "I shall never see you, may never hear of you, again. I know a priest's life is one of toil and hardship, especially in the new land, and his salary very small. It is my own, José," she implored, "do not refuse me. Take it, and think kindly of me, if you can." Touched by her thought, he promised, and should he never need to use it, he would leave it to the Church. Then, as she bowed her head, in broken accents, he called down Heaven's richest blessing on his loved one. Weeping bitterly, Dolores arose and left the confessional. As soon as he had recovered from his agitation, José left his seat, and entering the side of the confessional where Dolores had knelt, he saw an oblong parcel, wrapped in dark paper, lying on the floor far back in the corner. He took it up and carried it away with him. Not for many days after did he have the calmness to open it. Inside the wrapper was the wooden box we have already seen, on top of which lay a small, flat key. He unlocked the box, and with eyes full of tears, saw the glittering rows of gold coins, and the words traced by Dolores's pen.

But to-night Father Zalvidea decided to put the box in a safer place. Going to the window, and drawing aside the curtain, he opened it. Listening intently for a moment, and hearing nothing, he returned to the table, lighted a small dark lantern, extinguished the candle, and taking up the box after closing and locking it, he left the room, and walked softly through the passage out into the patio.

Aided by the feeble light from the moon, low down on the horizon, he hurried along the cloister to a room back of the church, which had been deserted and left to itself for many years, and was now almost in ruins. Going into one corner, Father Zalvidea, by the light of his lantern, found a small pick and shovel which, that afternoon, he had left there for this very purpose, and set to work to dig a hole in which to bury his treasure. Although the ground was hard, it required only a few minutes, after the cement floor was broken through, to accomplish this, for the box was small, and to bury it deep down was quite unnecessary. Father Zalvidea placed the box in the hole, covered it with the earth he had thrown to one side on a large sheet of paper he had brought with him, and then, carefully fitting together the pieces of cement he had broken, he sprinkled over it some of the remaining earth, to hide all traces of the disturbance—a thing very easy to do, as the cement was so nearly the color of the clay soil. Leaving the shovel and pick, he wrapped what earth was left in the paper, put it under his arm, took up the lantern, and wended his way back to his room, congratulating himself on having hidden the money safely.

Well would it have been for the Father, had he put his box of gold coins into the great, strong, securely padlocked chest standing in the vestry of the church, in which were kept the money and all the valuable articles—the gold embroidered vestments and the sacred vessels of silver—belonging to the mission. Father Zalvidea had, indeed, thought of it, but he had felt a strong repugnance to placing his own private property among that of the church; so, although much the better way, he had chosen the other. And how could he know there had been a pair of eyes watching him all the time he was busy in the deserted room? Such was the case, however, for a young *mestizo* had been witness of the whole proceeding. Juan, the seventeen year old son of a Mexican laborer, who had married one of the mission Indian women, united in himself the bad qualities of both races, as has so often been the result of such crosses. He had grown up idle, indifferent to his parents, vicious and cruel, leading astray the other youths of the mission, among whom he was easily the master, and causing his parents and Father Zalvidea no end of anxiety. The Father, in fact, had about made up his mind that Juan must be sent away to San Diego, and put under military discipline. To have him longer at liberty was not to be considered. This night Juan had been at the home of one of his boon companions, talking over the plans for a fandango to be given within a few days. Coming along leisurely by the wall of the building forming the east side of the patio, he saw the faintest glimmer of light shining through the opening of a ruined window. Standing on a stone, which he placed beneath the window, he looked in and saw the Father busily at work in the far corner of the room. Curiosity took possession of him, and he watched every movement of the worker until he had completed his task, taken up the lantern, and left the room. After waiting a few moments, to make sure he was not coming back, Juan sprang lightly through the window, and went to the corner where the Father had been occupied. First looking out into the patio to see that no one was there, he seized the shovel, and digging energetically a minute or two, struck the hard top of the box. Lifting it out he examined it by the moonlight coming in by the door, which he had left open. The box was heavy, but there was nothing else to indicate what were its contents. Juan knew the Father valued it, from the care with which he had secreted it, and surmised, from its weight, it might contain gold. Hastily filling the hole, and making the surface smooth as possible, in the dim light, he climbed out of the window, taking the box with him. Walking swiftly on the road for a half-mile farther, he came to a little adobe house where he and his parents lived. Passing the house, he hurried on to the garden and wheat-field belonging to his father, and, reaching the far end, he sat down on the ground and took the box in his lap to examine it at his ease. For a moment he hesitated, realising the magnitude of his crime, but only for a moment. He could not resist his curiosity to see the contents of the box; and, too, if it were gold, as he felt sure it must be, he intended to take it, for Juan had long had a great desire to run away to Mexico or Hawaii; but venturesome as he was, he could not quite bring himself to the point of carrying it out, for his indolence drew him back at the prospect of being obliged to work his way.

His hesitation quickly came to an end, and placing the box on the ground, he found a sharp stone, and began pounding it with quick, hard blows. Strong as the box was, it could not long withstand such treatment, and soon it fell apart, broken at the hinges. With a low cry of surprise, Juan gazed at the glittering coins; then, with feverish fingers, he took up a handful and examined them carefully, for he had never seen the Spanish *onza,* and did not know its value. That it was gold, however, satisfied him; he would find out its value later, for at the first sight of it, Juan had jumped at the fact that now he was a thief, and could not remain at the mission. With lightning speed he made up his mind to run away, and that very night. Two thousand dollars in gold is a heavy load for one's pocket, but that was the only way Juan could carry it, and he quickly transferred it to his two pockets. Not daring to go into the house, from fear of waking his parents, he set off, just as he was, for San Pedro, the nearest seaport, a walk of nearly fifty miles. But the box—he must not leave that lying on the ground in plain sight! He must take it with him until he could find some place to hide it, or throw it into the sea. He picked it up, and hurried off, not noticing the slip of paper, which had fallen out of the box when it was broken open. Walking all night, Juan found himself, at daybreak, still far from San Pedro, tired out and hungry. But he knew he must keep on, if he did not want to be overtaken and captured. We shall not follow him farther; it is more than certain he will be relieved of his gold, when he reaches San Pedro, by some friendly sailor or bad character of the settlement; and he will, after all, have to work his way to Mexico, for it would be out of the question to return to San Juan Capistrano.

Juan was frequently away for two or three days at a time, and his non-appearance the next morning caused no particular remark from his parents; and not until late in the afternoon of the second day of his absence did anything occur to lead them to think he was gone. His father had begun to cut his wheat the day before. This afternoon he was just finishing the last piece of the field, when he spied something white on the ground, almost hidden by the tall grain. Stopping his horse, he picked it up, wondering, and with some difficulty made out the writing on it. Where had it come from; to whom did it belong; who was Dolores—it was too much for his slow mind to fathom. But of one thing he was certain—it must be taken to the Father; he would know if it was of moment. And then it was he thought of his son and his absence. Hardly in his own mind did he connect it with the bit of paper; and yet the suspicion, once aroused, would not be dispelled. Finishing his work as quickly as possible, he returned to his house and told his wife what he had found, and then spoke of the absence of their son as, possibly, having some connection with it.

"I will take it to the Father to-morrow," said his wife, calmly, as became her race, but with an undertone of anxiety and sadness.

Early the next morning Juan's mother wended her way to the mission, and asking to see the Father, was led to his reception-room. He was sitting at a table covered with books and papers, reading from a large folio filled with the early statistics of the mission, the first few pages of which were written by the sainted Serra's hand. Father Zalvidea looked up as the Indian woman entered.

"Good morning, my daughter," he said. "What do you wish with me?"

The woman responded with a trembling voice, "Father, my husband found this in his wheat-field."

The Father took the paper with negligent curiosity. It was rumpled and dirty, far different from its appearance when in the box, and he did not recognise it. But as soon as he had smoothed it, and saw the handwriting, he sprang to his feet, crying:

"Woman, how came you by this? Tell me. Why did you bring it to me? Where is the box?"

Terrified at the outbreak she had evoked, the Indian fell on her knees before the priest, and exclaimed:

"Father, I know nothing more about it than what I have told you. My husband found it yesterday in his field, and gave it to me to bring to you. That is all, Father."

The Father composed himself with difficulty, and, after a moment, spoke with his accustomed calmness:

"My daughter, forgive me for speaking so harshly, and doubting your word, for I know you would not have brought me the paper if you had not come honestly by it. But I must see your husband at once."

The priest got his hat, and, accompanied by the woman, started quickly for her home.

Now the woman had said nothing about the suspicions her husband had had, and which he had imparted to her. However unworthy of her love, she was Juan's mother, and, Indian though she was, and with the inherited instincts of the savage, hers was the natural love found in civilised and savage alike, and she could not bring herself to tell the Father what she felt must be true. So, silently, the two hastened to her home. Juan's father was in the garden back of the house, weeding his vegetable patch. As soon as he saw his wife and the priest he came toward them.

"Pablo, tell me all you know about this paper?" said the Father abruptly, without preamble of any kind.

The man related the fact of his finding it, which was, indeed, all there was to tell. And then, with hesitation, spoke of Juan's absence.

The Father started.

"When did you see him last?" he asked.

"The day before yesterday, in the afternoon," replied the man. "He said he was going to see Fernando Diaz, who lives on the mission road, two miles north from here."

"Did you see him when he came back?" enquired the priest.

"No, Father," the man answered. "That is the last time we have seen him."

Father Zalvidea asked the man to show him the place where he had found the paper, and the two walked to the wheat-field. When they came to the spot, the Father looked carefully around on the ground, hoping to discover some trace of the box and its contents. Searching in the stubble, he did actually find one of the gold coins, but that was all. The box was too large to remain hidden in the field, and the Father knew it must have been carried away. He showed Pablo, who had been assisting in the search, the coin he had found, and then, as there was no object in concealment, told him of his loss.

The man's astonishment at the enormity of his son's offence was profound. He was struck dumb for some moments, but realising, at last, that his son was, in all likelihood, involved, he besought the Father to have pity on him.

"Pablo," said the priest, "have you no idea whither Juan is gone? Have you ever heard him say anything to lead you to think he wanted to leave the mission?"

"No, Father," he replied; for Juan always had been careful to say nothing of his longing to go to Mexico, as he knew he might be watched should he ever carry it out.

"I know not what to do," said the priest, "but I shall, at any rate, send messengers to San Diego and San Pedro. He might leave either place in some ship for Mexico or Central America, for he would not dare to go to San Luis Rey or San Gabriel, as he would be discovered and sent back. But I fear it will do no good."

The two returned to the house, where the woman still waited for them. She saw traces of emotion on the Father's face, and consternation written plainly on that of her husband, but, like a true Indian, asked no questions.

Father Zalvidea commanded the couple to say nothing about the matter, and returned to the mission. As soon as he reached it, he sent off two trusty neophytes, on horseback, one to San Diego, the other to San Pedro, with letters to friends in each place, relating the robbery. But no trace of Juan was found. He had had over two days' start, and by the time the messenger arrived at San Pedro, he was far out to sea in a ship which had sailed the very morning of the discovery of the theft.

After this cruel interruption, Father Zalvidea returned to his quiet life with a sorrowful heart. He did not regret the loss of the money, so far as he himself was concerned, for he had long destined it for the Church, as he knew he could retire to some monastery when too old and feeble for further usefulness; but the desecration of his secret was like a painful stab. The robbery had the effect, also, of calling forcibly to mind, once again, the life and love of other days—those halcyon days of youth, when all was sunshine and hope. During the rest of the day the Father was unable to control himself for any work whatsoever. He paced back and forth the length of his room; walked up and down the cloister surrounding the patio; wandered out around the garden, and even as far off as the bluff, a mile from the mission, from which could be seen the beach below, white with foam from the inrushing waves. It was many days before he regained his normal equanimity.

Father Zalvidea lived at Mission San Juan Capistrano nearly fifteen years after this episode in his life there. Two years after the robbery he heard that his loss was known to the mission. Pablo, while under the influence of too much *aguardiente,* had told of it. Father Zalvidea at once set to work to silence the gossip, and did so effectually, for he heard nothing more of it while he remained at the mission. But the rumor lived, although repressed, and for years after his departure, searches were made for the money which many believed had never been stolen, or, if recovered, had been reburied by the Father; for Pablo, babbling in his stupor, had not been careful as to accuracy. In fact, as late as 1888, there were people at San Juan Capistrano who still believed in the buried treasure, and explored the ruins of the mission, digging in various spots for it. Why the Father should have left his money buried there (supposing it not to have been stolen), instead of taking it with him when he removed from the mission, tradition does not state.

NOTE.—Bancroft: *History of California,* Vol. IV, p. 624, note, gives about all that is known of these famous *onzas* of Father Zalvidea. Probably it will never be known definitely what became of them.

In alluding to the earthquake of 1812, the writer has followed the commonly received assumption, derived from Bancroft, that it occurred December 8, and that this date fell on a Sunday. From later research, it is now believed to have occurred October 8, which was a Thursday. This seems more likely than the date given by Bancroft (December 8, 1812, fell on Tuesday), for he himself says forty of the attendants at mass were killed, the officiating priest and six others being all that were saved: he does not mention the wounded, if any. This would be far too small a number for a Sunday mass attendance.

LA BEATA

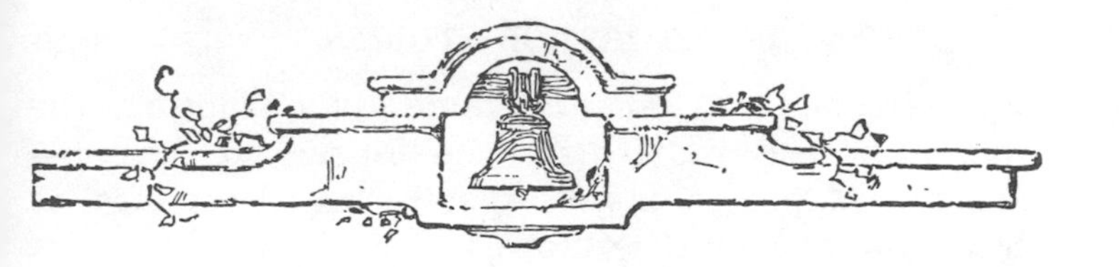

LA BEATA

IT WAS a bright summer morning in the month of June of the year 1798. All was bustle and excitement at the wharf in the harbor of the town of Acapulco, on the western coast of Mexico, for at noon a ship was to sail away for the province of Nueva California, in the far north. This was always an event to attract the attention of the town, partly from its infrequent occurrence, but more especially because, in those days, this northern Mexican province was an almost unknown land to the general mind. The first expedition to the new country, under the spiritual direction of the beloved Father Serra, had been sent out nearly thirty years before. But so many and conflicting were the tales of wars with the Indian natives, the struggles of the

Franciscans to make and maintain a footing, the hardships endured by all who journeyed thither—sometimes to the point of suffering the pangs of hunger—, and, on the other hand, the marvellous tales of the perfect climate, grand mountain ranges with snowy peaks, fertile soil nearly everywhere, there was a want of unanimous opinion respecting the northern land. Whenever, therefore, from time to time, a ship was sent from the mother country to her struggling colony, a great interest was always displayed. Each ship would be filled with agricultural produce of all kinds, implements of labor, clothing of every sort, including vestments and adornings for the mission churches, as well as laborers and soldiers, together, sometimes, with a few priests to swell the number already in the new field. The ship preparing for her voyage this pleasant June morning was the centre of all such busy scenes witnessed many times before, but which never seemed to lose their interest for the inhabitants of the town.

But this particular occasion was one of more than usual interest to the people assembled by the water to watch the preparations for departure. An hour before the time set for sailing, a procession was seen coming slowly down the main street of the town, heading for the ship. It was a strange, silent, pathetic little company. At the head were two sisters of charity, following them a score of young children, evenly divided as to sex, and all under ten years of age. They were dressed with the utmost simplicity, almost severity, although with extreme neatness.

Hardly a word was spoken among them as they came along, but their eyes were busy glancing from one side to the other, noting everything about them, and, in particular, the ship which was evidently their destination.

This little procession was the cause of the unusual interest shown in the sailing of the ship. The children were on their way from Mexico City to the new country, where they were to find homes among the people settled there; for they were foundlings, with no one but the Church to look to for aid in their helplessness. The Church had responded nobly, and had cared for these poor little waifs from infancy, and until they were large enough to be sent to their new home.

"Caramba!" exclaimed a by-stander to his companion. "What will become of the *pobrecitos* in that heathen country? I grow cold to think of it," he added with a shiver.

"Basta, Juan!" said his friend. "What do you know about it? Were it not for my wife and little one, I would go away quickly, and be glad to go. There are Indians here and in Baja California, plenty of them, and what harm do they do any one?"

"All very well," replied the other. "You may not believe it. But I have heard tales of that land which made my flesh creep. Know you not what the Indians did to Father Jaime at Mission San Diego? Would you like to have been there then? I think not."

"You remember well," answered his companion. "That was over twenty years ago. There are many more people there now, and the Indians would not dare do such things again. Besides, these children are going to Monterey, and that is a large town, I have heard."

The children boarded the ship, and were soon standing by the taffrail, watching the busy scene below, as the men hurried with the last loads of the cargo. Presently all was done, the vessel weighed anchor, and slowly making her way out of the harbor, set her course for the distant northern country.

During the three weeks' voyage these children lost much of their shyness at their strange surroundings, made friends with all on board, and had a generally royal good time—probably the first they had ever had in their short lives. Under charge of the sisters of the asylum whence they came, they had had the best of training, which, although lacking the individual love of the mother for her own children, was one to influence and increase their religious instincts, and to make them good, pious Catholic men and women. The children, almost without exception, were docile and obedient, venerating the sisters in charge, and quick to respond to their slightest word. Among the girls was one to be especially remarked, from her face and its habitual expression. Indistinguishable from the others in general appearance, it was only in glancing at her countenance that one thought to look at her a second time with close attention. She was not handsome, or even pretty, although not by any means homely; but her face was almost transfigured by its expression of earnest piety and goodness, remarkable in one so young. Quiet and sedate as was her habit, she was ever ready to enter freely into the fun and play of the other children; but even in the most absorbing frolic, if any one became hurt from too much roughness, she was the first to be on the spot to comfort the suffering one and to ease its pain.

Apolinaria Lorenzana (for so the child had been named by her guardians) had become the object of the love of the entire asylum, and of the sisters in charge of it, in particular. She was looked up to with respect, almost adoration, for her piety and devotion to all religious observances; and the sisters never tired of whispering to each other, prophesying what good works she would do during her life, led and taught by the Virgin as she most certainly was. The parting from her was a sore one to the sisters, more so than to Apolinaria herself, great as was her affection for them; but, in spite of her youth, she was already filled with her work in the new land to which she was going; and she was almost the only one of the little group of children to look forward with joy to the new life.

With fair winds, and under bright skies, the ship sped on her course, and, at the end of three weeks, cast anchor in the bay before the town of Monterey and opposite the presidio. Here the scenes enacted at their departure from Acapulco, were repeated, with even greater animation, although the number of people was pitifully small. It was touching to see the eagerness with which they welcomed the new-comers, strangers though they were; the passion with which they seized on letters from friends in Mexico, as soon as they were distributed; the interest shown in the news, extorted from each of the passengers, as they in turn were questioned, of everything which had occurred in their old home and in Spain, as well as in the rest of the world. Such was the hunger manifested by these home-sick persons! The children aroused quite as much interest here as they had on their departure, and with more reason, for this was to be their future home. Boys and girls stood on the deck, and noted everything going on. Such a little place Monterey seemed to these young people fresh from Mexico City—some dozen houses scattered here and there, a church, the Governor's house and the presidio, all of adobe, and all small and insignificant. But the little town made a pretty sight in the warm sunshine, with the bay and ocean in front, and the hills, forest-clad, behind.

During the height of the excitement incident to unloading, Governor Borica was seen to approach, accompanied by half a dozen soldiers from the presidio, and a Franciscan priest, who was come from the mission, six miles distant, to take charge of the little band of children, until they should be placed in permanent homes. Boarding the ship, the Governor and the Father made their way to the group, and greeted the two sisters, both of whom had been acquainted with the Governor before he left Mexico. The children, instructed by the sisters, made a deep obeisance to the Governor, and kneeled before the Father, as he spoke to each in turn. A few minutes later all left the ship, and the priest, with the sisters and children, set out, on foot, for the mission. The way was long, but no one thought of fatigue; for it lay, for the most part, along the edge of the shore, with the ocean in full sight, the waves dashing on to the rocks strewn thickly here and there, while now and then the scene was varied with clusters of cypress trees growing in fantastic shapes. It was past noon when they reached the mission, a small establishment, having, at this time, about eight hundred Indians, under the charge of the Father and his assistants.

The children, however, did not remain here long. During the next two weeks homes were found for them, some among the families at Monterey, some were sent across the bay to Mission Santa Cruz, and some as far as Mission Santa Clara; so that, by the end of that time, not one was left at Mission San Carlos, the two sisters alone continuing there to give their aid in all manner of work looking toward the betterment of the Indians.

Among the children finding homes in Monterey was Apolinaria. Pleased with her appearance, when he saw her at the disembarkation, Don Raimundo Carrillo, a well-known and powerful personage in the new country, decided to take her into his own family, consisting of himself, his wife and three small children. This was a piece of rare good fortune for Apolinaria, for Señor Carrillo was noted for his kind heart to all inferiors; and with this family she found a home than which none could have been happier in the whole colony. Apolinaria was not adopted by the

Carrillos—she filled, in some measure, the place of a servant, while, at the same time, she was regarded as one of the family in all domestic relations, and became a companion, in many respects, to Señora Carrillo, who was an invalid. And beyond all this, Apolinaria was under the religious charge of the mission fathers, as were all the foundlings brought to the province. The fathers not only instructed and admonished them in the Catholic faith, but kept informed as to the temporal welfare of their every-day life.

And now began a time of happiness for Apolinaria; busy all day, sometimes at the roughest toil, she worked with her whole heart, full of joy because she was busy, and was doing something for the good people with whom she had found a home. But more than this: the change from her old shelter in the asylum in the great city to a life in the sweet, wild new country, beautiful with all that was loveliest in nature, was one to make a character like Apolinaria expand and grow into a rounded simplicity of soul and spirit. Father Pujol had heard of Apolinaria's piety on her coming to Monterey, having a chance, also, of observing it during her short stay at the mission; and he watched over her with more than usual interest, instructing her mentally, as occasion offered, in addition to fostering the religious side of her nature. Apolinaria attended the school in the town until she was thirteen years old, and acquired the elements of an education, as much as she could possibly have any occasion to use in after years in the country whither she was come for life.

As Apolinaria grew older, and after she had ceased going to school, she found, even with her accustomed duties in Don Raimundo's home, that she had much unoccupied time; and with her religious fervor she thought long on the matter, trying to find in what way she could more completely fill the place she believed the Holy Virgin had destined for her. But in vain did she seek for this object; and at length arose slowly in her, becoming more and more fixed as she dwelt on it, the thought that maybe she had been mistaken in considering that a life in Nueva California was meant for her; and with the thought was awakened the longing to return to Mexico and become a nun. This was during her fifteenth year. A young girl with her religious habit of mind would, naturally, turn to the convent, and regard a life spent in it as the worthiest, therefore the most desirable, to be found in this sinful world; and Apolinaria, notwithstanding her strength of character, soon became fascinated with the prospect. She thought long and seriously before saying a word to any one; for much as she now wished it, she knew it would be painful both to herself and to the good Carrillos, and she dreaded to disclose her plan. But at last, believing she had definitely decided that it concerned the future welfare of her soul, she betook herself to her spiritual adviser, Father Pujol, and laid her thought before him.

Now Father Pujol was a man—one of many in this imperfect world—who had not found his proper place in life. His father had intended to take him, as a partner, into business, toward which he had a natural leaning, so soon as he was of sufficient age; but Señor Pujol suffered reverses which swept away his modest fortune, and left his family destitute. Rather than receive aid from his uncle, and waiving his claim in favor of his younger brother, this son, although with reluctance, decided to enter the priesthood, for he was a singularly religious young man. But Father Pujol, in his capacity as priest, combined, in a marked degree, the wisdom of the serpent with the harmlessness of the dove. He had a deeply rooted aversion to the custom of women sequestering themselves from the world behind the walls of a convent; and it had been his habit, whenever opportunity offered, to dissuade any who, by so doing, might leave a void in the world. Indeed, he had been so zealous in one or two cases that the suspicions of his fellow-brethren had been aroused, and, eventually, he was selected to make one of a company of Franciscans to the new province. Therefore, on hearing for the first time what Apolinaria meditated doing, he felt almost angry with her, foolish and unreasonable though he knew he was.

"My blessed child!" he exclaimed, "what has made you think of such a thing?"

"I know not, Father," replied Apolinaria, "but it seemed to have been put into my mind by the saints in Heaven that that was what I should do; and I believe that must be what I was destined for when I was found by the dear sisters, forsaken and starving, and was taken to the asylum. Did not they save my life that I might glorify God and the Blessed Virgin the rest of my days?"

"Listen, Apolinaria," replied the Father solemnly. "I know well the state of your mind concerning this question. I have no word of blame to give you, and I am sure that the life you would pass in the convent would be acceptable to God; one, indeed, of good work done for others, in so far as your limited sphere of action would permit. But, my dear child, consider carefully before you decide to take this step, whether it may not be a step backward in your progress toward a heavenly home. Here you are, a member of a leading family in Nueva California, in the midst of duties which you can, and do, discharge faithfully, and which would not be done so well by any one else, should you give them up. Think of the help and comfort you are to Señora Carrillo, in her poor health, with three children, who would be a sad burden to her without you. Look at the place you fill in the household, where you are, in truth, the housekeeper. Is not your life full of good work? What more could you find in a convent? I know, my daughter, you wish for the life of devotion to be found there, and that you look on it as a life of rapture and uplifting. That is all very well for many poor women who have no especial sphere of usefulness to fill in the world; but, Apolinaria, I should deeply mourn the day that saw you become one of them. Do not think I am decrying the convent—far be from me such a thing! But I believe, I know, God never intended that his creatures should isolate themselves in any such way from the duties among which He had placed them."

The Father had risen to his feet as he uttered the last sentence, and, with some agitation, took a few steps back and forth in the room. He was an earnest, deep-souled man, eager and passionate, almost to the point of inspiration, when aroused from his usual reserved manner. Apolinaria was greatly beloved by him, and it was with genuine pain that he had heard her wish.

"Apolinaria," he said at last, after a few moments of silence on the part of both, "*hija mia,* have I made you see this matter clearly? Can not you trust me to decide this weighty question for you? Is your heart so set on the quiet life of prayer, cut off from so much of the work, without which, Saint James tells us, faith is dead? Do not decide now," he added, as Apolinaria made an uncertain attempt to speak, "take plenty of time, daughter; think it over during the next week, and then come to see me again and let me know."

"I thank you, Father, and I shall consider what you have said to me. Will you pray for me that I may be guided aright?"

"Surely, my daughter," replied the Father, and laying his hands on her head as Apolinaria knelt before him, continued in slow, measured tones: "May the Mother of God help you to choose that which will ever be most pleasing and acceptable to her Son, our Lord Jesus Christ."

"Amen," whispered Apolinaria.

During the next few days Apolinaria thought of Father Pujol's words. It was a great disappointment to her to give up her long-cherished plan; but from the moment of leaving the Father she knew in her heart what the outcome would be. Yet it cost her a pang of regret as she thought of the quiet walls in Mexico which she used to look upon with a hush of awe, and dream of the lives of peace and holiness passed behind them. But she was not one to grieve long over what cost some tears to resign, and soon was, heart and soul, absorbed once more in whatever her hand found to do. Father Pujol having suggested the plan to her, she now, for the first time, took up the study of nursing at the mission hospital, instructed by the two sisters who had come with her and the other children some years before, and who had remained at the mission. There were always many patients among the neophytes, and here Apolinaria found a work ready to her hand, which soon claimed all the time she could give to it. This was an intense happiness to her, and the Father saw, with the utmost satisfaction, that his remedy was a good one.

Not long after this Señor Carrillo was called to Santa Bárbara to take command of the presidio, and knowing he should be kept there for many months, perhaps years, he decided to move his family to this new place of activity, and make it his future home. Apolinaria alone, of all the household, was averse to the change. She had just given herself unreservedly to her work with calm, patient enthusiasm, that left no room for regretful thought for what she had once longed to do; she could not bear the idea of parting from Father Pujol, who had been, indeed, a father to her, and who had had so much influence in marking out her life work. It was with tears she said the last bitter "adios" to him, on the eve of the departure; for in those days and in that country, there could be no probability that she would ever see him again, less likely in this case, as Father Pujol was far on life's decline. But even Apolinaria's sorrow at leaving Monterey could not destroy the interest and pleasure felt on arriving at Santa Bárbara, one of the most beautiful places in the province, and at that time much larger than Monterey. As the ship came into the roadstead which served as a harbor, the town lay spread out before them: in the foreground, straggling along the beach and for some distance back, were the adobe houses of the inhabitants, about one hundred in number, most of them glittering white in the brilliant sunlight; among them, somewhat distant from the shore, was the huge, low building of the presidio, frowning out over the rest of the scene; beyond the houses, and nearly two miles from the water, was the mission, a large group of buildings, from the midst of which rose the white two-towered Moorish church. Back of all was the long range of mountains, stretching off far into the north, in color a wonderful changing golden pink, streaked with palest blue-grey in the shadows. It was a perfect picture of peace, the sole hostile point in the whole being the presidio, which served but to accentuate the quiet beauty of the rest.

Even when the passengers were landed from the ship, the quiet of the town was not disturbed in any great degree. It was only when a vessel from Mexico arrived, when the Governor of the province visited them, or when news of an Indian uprising was brought, that the town awoke from its almost lethargic calm. All this Apolinaria found out later. Today, however, the undisturbed quiet of the place suited her best, and she would not have had it otherwise, surprised as she was at first to find it thus, so different from the bustle attending any event, even the slightest, occurring at Monterey. Don Raimundo and his family were domiciled in the home of Captain José de la Guerra, a friend of his, who met him at the landing to render all the assistance in his power. The captain's house was a large one, and Don Raimundo was led to this plan on account of the growing infirmity of his wife.

It did not require a long while for a quiet soul like Apolinaria to take up once more in the new home the broken threads of her life; and before she had been there many days, she had found more than enough to employ all her time. At Monterey Apolinaria had been in part servant, in part mistress of the household, discharging the duties of her somewhat anomalous position. In Santa Bárbara, on the contrary, her services as domestic and housekeeper were dispensed with, and she was at liberty to give her whole time and attention to the occupation which she had but just begun to pursue at Monterey. She offered her services to the priests at the mission as a nurse for the sick neophytes in the hospital. The winter before had been a severe one for the health of the Indian community, and there had been an unusual number of cases of smallpox—the most common disease with which they were afflicted. Capable nurses were hard to find, and the fathers gladly accepted Apolinaria's offer. Once her qualities becoming known and appreciated, she was in almost constant demand from one end of the town to the other, for she displayed a skill in the care of the sick that came from born aptitude.

Here Apolinaria remained for several years, engrossed in her work which had now taken complete possession of her. As she became better known, she had calls from many high caste Spanish residents who desired her services, and not only those living in Santa Bárbara, but in near-by towns—San Buenaventura, Santa Inés, and as far as Los Angeles; and her fame reached, at last, the whole length of the chain of settlements in the province, from San Diego to San Francisco, for she was the sole person in that part of the country who undertook the office of what is now filled by the trained nurse. After a time, Apolinaria, finding there was room for many more like herself, gathered a few young women into a class whom she taught what she knew in regard to nursing the sick, and upon whom she called for such assistance as they were able to give.

One morning a mission neophyte came to her with a message from Father Amestoy, that he desired to see her as soon as she could come to him. Wondering a little at the seeming urgency of the request, she took her way to the mission at the end of her morning's visit to the hospital. She met the Father walking slowly up and down in front of the monastery, every now and then looking off down the road with anxious impatience. As soon as he saw Apolinaria approaching, he hurried to meet her.

"My child," he exclaimed, "you are come at last! I have been watching for you the whole morning."

"I could not come before, Father," she replied. "Did you want me at once?"

"Yes, Apolinaria," the Father answered. "Late last night a messenger came from San Diego with a letter from Father Barona, imploring us to send you down there. They are in great trouble. The smallpox is raging; so many neophytes are ill that help is needed to care for them. The fathers are worn out with watching and tending the dying, and burying the dead, and all the Spaniards are too occupied with their own sick to be of much assistance. They want you to come. Will you go, Apolinaria?"

"Most assuredly, Father," Apolinaria replied promptly. "I shall be ready to start to-morrow at daybreak. I cannot leave sooner for I must give last directions to my pupils. But how shall I go? Have you made arrangements for me?"

"You can return with the messenger. I shall give him full instructions. With hard riding you can reach there in three days. Do you think you can stand it? I would not ask it did not they need you so badly—just as soon as you can get there."

"Do not think of me, Father. I shall not fail."

After a few more words Apolinaria left the mission, and returning to the town, made preparations for her absence, which bade fair to be a prolonged one. Bitter regrets were felt and expressed by the people, some going so far as to mutter against the priest for sending her, for "does not Apolinaria belong to us, and why should we, how can we, spare her to go so far away for a lot of sick Indians?"

The next morning, an hour before the sun was up, Father Amestoy and the messenger, each with a horse from which they had dismounted, stood at Apolinaria's door. In a moment Apolinaria came out of the little adobe house which had been her abode since leaving the Carrillos, bearing a small bundle in her arms. Kneeling before the Father, he gave her his blessing, and then asked her abruptly if she was ready to start.

"Yes, Father, I am quite prepared."

"Then you must be off at once," he replied. "I have given the messenger instructions for your journey. You have swift horses. If possible, get to San Fernando to-night; that is the longest day's ride you will have, but if too much for you, or if you be delayed on the way, stop at some rancho this side for the night. In that case your ride to-morrow will be longer, for you ought to get to Mission San Juan by to-morrow night; from there to San Diego is a short distance compared with the others. You will change horses at San Buenaventura, and at the ranchos on the way from there to San Fernando. Felipe knows where to stop for them. He has letters also for the padres at the missions, and will see to everything. And now, my daughter, may the saints protect you and keep you, and bring you back once more to your friends here, when you shall be no longer needed at San Diego."

When the Father had ceased speaking, he assisted Apolinaria to mount her horse, and with a last "adios" she made off, preceded by the messenger, who had taken her bundle and fastened it to his saddle. The priest watched them as they hurried away in a cloud of dust, and then, breathing a blessing for Apolinaria, returned to the mission.

It was a glorious June morning. The air was fresh and crisp; the water was just taking on a tinge of yellow from the light of the yet unrisen sun, and the sky above was of the intensest blue. The road, for the first twenty miles, lay along the shore, now on the beach itself, the water not seldom lapping the horses' feet, now on the mesa above. Open to all impressions of the beautiful in nature as was Apolinaria, she had little time, or, indeed, inclination, for its indulgence this morning, for the messenger had set the pace at a hard gallop, and her attention was taken up with the riding. She was a good horsewoman, and found no difficulty in keeping up with Felipe, although, whenever they came to a bit of bad road, he slackened his pace a little. The sun was not two hours high when they reached San Buenaventura, where they were received by the fathers, given fresh steeds, and were soon on their way again. With the exchange of horses they kept up their speed, and as the hours went by, the riders saw mile after mile left behind. Whenever they stopped for horses at the ranchos lying on the road, they were welcomed by all, and to Apolinaria was shown the greatest deference, and everything was done to make her long ride as little fatiguing as possible, for her fame was known to all, as well as the reason for her present journey. Thus the day passed. Toward noon Apolinaria began to feel the effects of her rapid flight, but she had no thought of stopping, for she was determined to reach San Fernando that night. Slowly the day wore by, and the miles slipped behind them; but the sun was set, and night was over them before they reached San Fernando. Two miles before arriving, they met a horseman who had been sent out on the road to meet them, in case, as the padres hoped, Apolinaria should come that night. At last they reached the mission, where Apolinaria was welcomed warmly. But she was too exhausted to do more than eat a little, drink a cup of chocolate, and then retire for the night, which she passed in a heavy, dreamless sleep.

The next morning she was up with the first faint grey of dawn, although she was so stiff and lame that every movement caused her agony; but this wore off gradually as soon as she set out once more after breakfast with the fathers. We shall not follow her journey in detail. The second day was easier as she had only seventy-five miles to cover to reach San Juan Capistrano. At Capistrano she found the first traces of the epidemic, a few of the Indians being ill with the smallpox. At Mission San Luis Rey there were a much larger number, and at all of the settlements in the region were many patients, but only at the southernmost mission were the people in great straits. In the afternoon of the third day Apolinaria arrived at her destination, tired out, but happy to be, at last, where she was so much needed. Here she found a scene of desolation: more than half of the neophyte population down with the fell disease; the two fathers used up with the care of their especial work; the few Mexican women available for nurses without a head to take charge of affairs at the hospital. Apolinaria, forgetting her fatigue from the long, hard ride, set to work at once where she was most needed, in the hospital; and with her skill and experience she, in a few days, wrought a wonderful change. It was a simple matter, after all, and the fathers had acted wisely in sending for her, as she supplied what was lacking—a head; and after she had fitted herself into her proper place, everything went on smoothly, and Apolinaria and her assistants were able to cope with the plague successfully.

One morning, while it was still at its height, Apolinaria, on making her visit for the day to the hospital, found a new patient. He was a soldier from the presidio, six miles away, who had developed symptoms of the disease, and had been dismissed and sent to the mission hospital, while he was yet able to bear the journey; a handsome young man, hardly more than a youth, with all the fire, vivacity and pride of the Spaniard, tempered in his case with a touch of sadness, lending an indefinable charm to his countenance. It was an attractive face, and so Apolinaria found it; but with a second glance at the young soldier, she had an uneasy feeling that she had seen him before. She had met so few people in her life, that it was not difficult for her to remember the youth as one of her young companions from the asylum in Mexico, who had come with her to Nueva California nearly fifteen years before. But if she was a little slow in placing the stranger in her memory, he, on the contrary, as soon as his eyes rested on her, showed, by the lighting up of his countenance, that he already knew and recognised her. As she approached he held out his hand, crying eagerly:

"Apolinaria, *tu me recuerdas* (You remember me)?"

"Surely, Pedro, how could I forget one of those who were so large a part of my life in the old days? But little did I expect to see you here, and it grieves me sorely to find you ill."

"That is a little thing, Apolinaria, after many of the hardships I have been through since we came to this country. But I shall not talk of that. It is a hard land for all who come. Tell me of yourself, Apolinaria. Have you found many trials? But I think you can have none now, for though you work hard, you must be very happy with it all. You see I have heard much about you, and the good you have done in these last years."

"Another time maybe, Pedro," Apolinaria replied, "but you are here to get well, and I cannot stop now to talk. I must make my rounds. I shall see you again, for I come here every day."

And Apolinaria left him hastily to visit another room of the hospital. His gaze followed her until she was out of sight; then, slowly closing his eyes, he leaned back in his chair.

The next day he was too ill to leave his bed. His attack was not severe, but the disease seemed to leave him without strength to recover, and many days passed before he began to improve. During all the time, Apolinaria visited him once or twice every day, and it was not long before Pedro learned to know her hours for the hospital, and to watch and wait for her coming. If, for any reason, she was delayed in her daily visit to him, he fretted nervously until she appeared. Now this, to one in his condition, is dangerous, but how could poor, simple Pedro know it? So he gave himself to his one happiness of the moment, without suspicion of whither it was leading him. The nurses in the hospital soon noticed his interest in Apolinaria, but mistook the direction it was taking.

"How can I help loving her?" he said, in response to some remark made to him. "Saw you ever any one so beautiful as she? I could pray to her as I do to the Holy Virgin, for I think she is as good. She is *una beata,* is she not?"

And those who heard what he said were of one mind on this point, and the title thus given to Apolinaria by the man who loved her, was, ere long, the one by which she became known to all—La Beata.*

But before Pedro had entirely recovered from his illness, he realised the nature of his fondness for

* Literally, the blessed one; a woman who gives herself to works of charity.

Apolinaria. Dismayed and perplexed, he knew not what to do, for, to tell his love for her seemed to his simple eyes an impertinence. That he should dare to love one so immeasurably above him—one in whom earthly love was merged in her love for God and her fellowmen! No, he must go back to his old life at the presidio, just as soon as he was able, and leave her with his love unsaid.

But love sometimes is stronger than will, and so it proved in Pedro's case. He determined to leave the mission the next day, without a word to any one, and this last evening he had wandered out into the olive orchard near the church. It was the close of a hot summer day, toward the end of June; the sun was just set in the glowing western sky, and all nature seemed to take a breath of relief in the cool evening air. Pedro had been there only a few moments when Apolinaria appeared, approaching from the river beyond the orchard, where she had been to see some of her patients. Pedro, undecided whether to stay quiet and risk a last meeting with her, or, as prudence whispered, to flee, hesitated too long, and she was close to him before he awoke from his indecision. She did not see him, in the fast gathering dusk, until close to the spot where he was standing.

"You here, Pedro!" she exclaimed. "But it is not well to be out at this time of the day. Don't you know you are doing wrong? I am astonished to see you so careless," she added, smiling.

It was the first time Pedro had seen her smile in any but a grave, quiet way. Now, accompanied as it was with the half-playful, half-deprecating manner in which she uttered her chiding, it proved too much for him.

"*Doña,*" he said, "I am going away to-morrow. I have struggled hard to leave here without showing you my heart, and I should have done so had not you come by this way to-night. Oh, why are you so far above me, that I must think of you as one belonging to Heaven rather than earth? Why are you so good and beautiful? For know, *Doña,* I love you, I love you," and Pedro poured out his confession of love in a swift rushing stream of words.

Amazed at such vehemence in one who had always until now shown himself the quietest of mortals, Apolinaria listened, as in a dream, hardly comprehending the full significance of what she heard. At last, with a start, she gave a slight shiver, and interrupted Pedro in the midst of his impassioned speech.

"Pedro," she said gently and quietly, "I am sorry you have told me this, more sorry you should have allowed such a feeling toward me to take root and grow up in you, for I am sure, my friend, you will see that I could not entertain any such change in my life as is implied in your words. Once, when I was younger than I am now, and before I had taken up my special work, I may have had dreams of a home and love as you are now experiencing; but it was only for a short time, for, I thought, 'who would choose a poor outcast foundling for a wife?' I will tell you how I came to take up the work I have been doing these years;" and Apolinaria related her youthful desire to enter a convent, and how she was led to give herself to her present active work. This she did, partly because she felt it was only just to Pedro, partly because she wished to lead him away from again bringing up the subject of his love.

Pedro listened absently to her story. The fire had died out of his heart with the uttering of his confession, for he knew, even before he began, how hopeless it all was. How could such an one as Apolinaria, engrossed and absorbed in her work, but raised far above this life and its passions, think of so poor and humble a being? He had been overpowered with the intensity of his emotion, and, his resolution broken, he had hurried on, knowing, poor fool that he was, the hopelessness and folly of it. Like a sudden, severe storm, coming after a day of intense, sultry heat, leaving the air refreshed, and the birds singing melodiously their evening hymns, so it was with Pedro. After his wild outburst, he was once more the quiet, reserved young man he had shown himself to be—the same, yet with a difference, for his love for Apolinaria had an effect on him that he felt all his life. She became to him an example which he followed willingly and joyfully, on their journey toward the life beyond.

When Apolinaria concluded her tale, a silence of some minutes fell upon the two, broken by the plaintive cry of an owl as it flew softly overhead toward the church. At last Apolinaria awoke from the revery into which she had fallen, and speaking brightly and cheerfully, but with a tender accent, said:

"You must go in, Pedro, and I have a sick woman to visit before I finish my day's work. I shall not see you again, *amigo mio,* but I shall not forget you, believe me. Live a good life and be happy."

And saying this, she held out her hand. Pedro bent low and kissed it reverently, without a word. Then, after one long, steady look into her face, he turned abruptly, and walked slowly through the orchard and back to the mission. The next morning he was gone.

Apolinaria continued with her nursing at San Diego for some weeks longer, until the disease had done its worst, and then returned to Santa Bárbara. But after this she never was allowed to remain there for long at a time. From San Diego to San Luis Obispo, and beyond, she was in demand; and whenever a wish for her assistance was sent to her, she always responded. Not infrequently, more than one mission would implore her presence. Then she would visit the one most in distress, and send some of her pupils to the others. Thus she passed her days in good work toward her fellowmen, finding her reward in the blessing of God which crowned her life. And ever after her first visit to San Diego, she was called by the name which Pedro, in his love, had bestowed upon her—La Beata.

JUANA

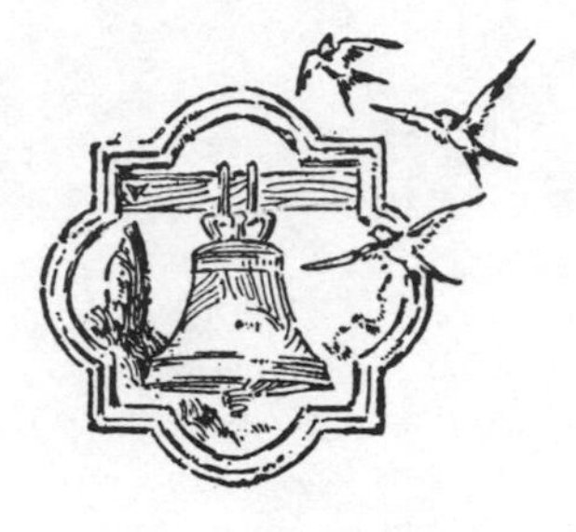

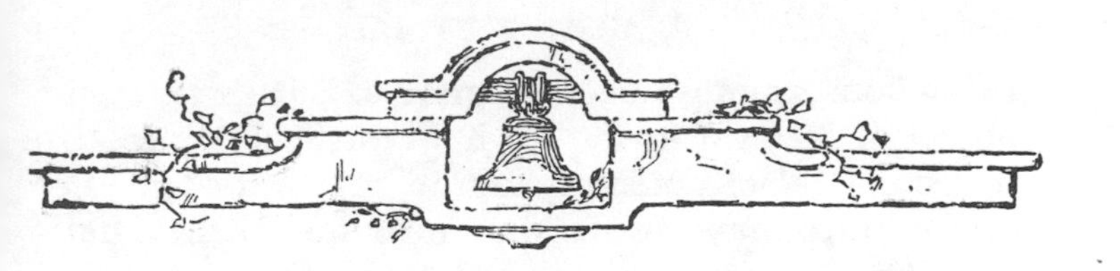

JUANA

THE overland mail-train from San Francisco, on the way to New Orleans, came to a stop for a minute or two at the little old town of San Gabriel, ten miles east of Los Angeles. It was a hot July afternoon, in the year 1890; the car windows were open, and the passengers were gazing out listlessly at the few signs of animation about the station and town. San Gabriel is a sleepy old place, with little to interest the ordinary person. A traveller, passing through it, sees nothing to attract his notice as the train pauses at the station, and he finds his gaze wandering off to the north, where it meets the lofty San Gabriel Mountains, a long line of blue-grey, shimmering in the heat of the plains. There is much beautiful scenery around San Gabriel, and wonderful cañons among these mountains. But there is one object of interest in the town we must not forget to mention—the old mission church, which the traveller on the train may see standing near the track, a half-mile before coming to the station. It is a fine old structure, planted firmly and solidly on the ground, and looking as though it might stand another century, without showing more marks of age than it does now after having closed its first one hundred years. This is an object in which every passer-by, even the most indifferent, finds an interest.

The engine panted, the passengers gazed absently at the men exchanging the bags of mail. All at once a sound of singing was heard in the distance. It was a woman's voice, old and quavering, and the song was a weird, almost unearthly, chant or dirge in a minor key. Slowly the singer approached the station, and reaching it, mounted the steps of the platform and seated herself on a bench, keeping on, without pause, her monotonous singing. The woman was a Mexican, very poorly dressed, and looked to be all of ninety years of age. This aroused in some slight degree the interest of the passengers.

"Who is that old woman?" asked one, of a brakeman who stood by his window.

"Oh," laughed the man, "that is old Jane. She is here nearly every day, when the train comes in."

"What is the matter with her? Is she crazy?" asked the traveller.

"Yes," answered the brakeman.

There was no time for more. The conductor called

"all aboard," and the train moved slowly away, leaving the old woman still intoning her chant.

The year 1824 opened with a feeling of distrust and uneasiness affecting all the missions of Nueva California, from San Juan Capistrano northward to Monterey. The fathers had held communication with each other many times regarding the Indians in their charge, and it was confessed by all that trouble from them was to be feared. At the same time nothing of any tangible import had occurred to lead the mission fathers to this conclusion. A few insubordinate individuals among the neophytes had been a little more insubordinate than usual; several had run away from Santa Inés and Purísima to their old haunts and companions in the mountains; some indications of a revival of the superstitious religious customs of the Indians had been discovered; once, at San Luis Obispo, among the neophytes living at some distance from the mission, a dozen men had been found, one night, by a Mexican servant of the fathers, preparing some poison with which to tip the points of their arrows. This last was ominous, and carried more weight than all the other signs of trouble brewing, and roused the fathers to some activity; for the neophytes, at that late day, in mission history, were not allowed to envenom their arrows without the express sanction of the fathers. But nothing could be learned from the disobedient Indians when they were questioned. They maintained that they were preparing for the hunting and killing of some large and fierce bears which had been seen in the neighborhood, and which had destroyed some of their cattle. They were permitted to keep the arrows, with a reprimand, and a strict watch on their movements was held for many days. Nothing definite could be discovered, however, and the fathers were forced to wait, with anxiety and added watchfulness, for whatever was to come.

There had been many false alarms, ever since the first settlement of the country, and many slight uprisings of the Indians, who saw, with disfavor, their land taken from them, and themselves obliged to serve almost as slaves, at the missions. They were nearly always well-treated, and, in fact, were usually tractable, and even more than satisfied with their lot; but now and then they would be roused by some of the fiercer spirits among them to struggle against this slavery. At such times, the injury they could, and did, inflict on the missions was great, but they had always been subdued and forced back to their state of servitude. Yet the fathers had ever with them this condition of anxiety, rendered all the greater as the military force in the country was very small, and usually unavailable at the moment when needed, owing to the distance between their barracks and the larger number of the missions.

Not quite three miles from Mission San Gabriel, toward the mountains in the north, stood a little adobe house, the home of a young Mexican, one of the men belonging to the mission, with his wife and one year old child. Diego Borja, this was the man's name, had been connected with the mission ever since he was a boy, serving in various occupations, first, as altar boy, then as occasion required, as messenger and servant to the Father, carpenter, for he was a skilled artisan, and overseer of the planting and gathering of the crops. He had even been trusted by the Father with commercial negotiations with merchants at San Pedro and Los Angeles, selling to them hides, which were a valuable source of wealth to the mission, and wine, famous for its fine quality. He was, in fact, a general utility man, on whom, on account of his reliability and versatile qualities, the Father depended greatly. Father Zalvidea, the senior priest at San Gabriel, had reason to congratulate himself on having Diego at his command, for not often is such an one found among the poorer and laboring class of Mexicans, combining the power and ability to serve in manifold ways, with a love of work for its own sake as well as for the reward it brings—very different from the general slowness and laziness of this class.

Two years before this little tale opens, Diego had become attached to a young girl living at the mission. Juana was an orphan, and had come to Nueva California from the same institution in Mexico which, many years before, had sent "La Beata," well known and loved by every one in the country. Juana had none of the characteristics of the celebrated Apolinaria, excepting only her piety, for she was a simple young woman, doing what was given her to do with a devout, unquestioning thankfulness, happy that she was able to work for those who had befriended her.

She had been at San Gabriel for some years, and was the teacher of the Indian girls' school. It was the most natural thing to occur in the little world at San Gabriel, that Diego and Juana should be drawn to each other, for neither had any relatives at the mission, and it happened that there were no other Mexicans of their own age here at this time. It was with much hesitation that Diego had told the Father of his love, for the priest, although one of the kindest of men, disliked change of any sort, were it the most trivial, a condition due as much to temperament as to age, although the Father was now past the meridian of life. Diego's great desire was to have a home for himself and his wife away from the mission, for he was tired of the communal life which he had lived for twenty years. Nothing but the love and respect he had for Father Zalvidea, and the knowledge that he was, in a measure, necessary to him, had kept him from making the change long before. But at last he was resolved to hazard the matter, and with his mind made up, he broached the subject one evening, after having received the priest's orders for the following day.

The Father's surprise was great, for, somewhat strangely, the thought that the relations between himself and Diego might be altered or broken had never occurred to him; yet not so strangely, after all, for after having had his services for nearly twenty years, what more natural than his coming to regard the existing arrangement to be impossible of change? Yet why should Diego's marriage make any difference in the present condition of things? Married or single, would not Diego and Juana continue to live at the mission? And so, somewhat to Diego's surprise, the Father offered no remonstrance to his wish.

But when Diego asked him if he might have a piece of the mission land where he could build a house, and make his home, the Father exclaimed:

"My son, are you dissatisfied with your life here? Must you leave me, and give up all your old occupations at the mission? Cannot you and Juana be contented here? What shall I do without you, for you are my right hand man, and there is no one here I could trust to take your place?"

"Father," replied Diego, "I should be sorry to feel obliged to give up doing all in my power for you and the mission; nor would I. I do not wish to go far. The land I want is less than three miles away, and I could be here at your command almost as much of the time as now. But if it be wrong to desire a place of my own, which I can plant and cultivate, and make of it a home, I will not ask it."

"No, Diego," answered the Father, "it is not wrong to wish for such a thing, nor can I say you nay. I am no longer young, although, I thank God, still strong to labor for many years yet, I hope, for our Mother Church. But I shall let you do as you like. You have been a good servant to me, Diego, and I will not withhold from you your reward."

Diego had selected a piece of ground of about ten acres, situated north of the mission, and near the foot-hills leading up to a cañon of the San Gabriel

Mountains. A line of shrubs and small trees cut diagonally across the land, marking the course of a rivulet, which, not a half-mile farther, lost itself in the light, dry sand of the plain. This tiny stream would suffice for irrigation, and it was the particular feature that had decided Diego to choose this place. He at once set about clearing the land and building the house. With the Father's permission for everything needed, he soon had a number of neophytes busily at work making adobes, and building the walls under his supervision. Houses were quickly built in Nueva California in those days. They were but plain, simple structures at best, and, at the missions, an unlimited number of workmen took only a few days to finish one.

Diego and Juana had a grand wedding. Both favorites of the Father, and Diego, in particular, whom he regarded rather as friend than servant, the priest made it a holiday, and the mission church was crowded to the doors, in the morning, at the marriage ceremony. In the afternoon the Indians and the Mexicans celebrated the day with a bull-fight, horse racing, and various games and diversions, Mexican and aboriginal. The day was one long remembered by all the inhabitants of the mission.

The newly wedded couple took up their abode in the tiny adobe house Diego had built, and began a life of great happiness, little disturbed by affairs outside their own domain. Life in California, in those days, was a *dolce far niente* kind of existence that was most captivating, although ruffled at times by troubles with the many Indians on all sides. The days sped by, each one making but the slightest notch in the span of life. Juana continued her teaching, riding to the mission every day, where she spent the morning. During the rest of the day, after returning home, she busied herself about the house in all domestic duties, or in embroidering, at which she was an adept, her work being much in request, not only at San Gabriel, but at the other missions; or in tending her garden, where were growing many vegetables and fruits for their use. The birth of their child brought an added joy to their already overflowing life of happiness. But this kind of life could not last forever, even in that idyllic land of Nueva California.

Diego was given the services of two neophytes in cultivating his land, leaving him at liberty to continue those of his mission duties which could not be delegated to another. And toward the end of the second year of Diego's married life, his presence at the mission became more urgent, and he was sent off to the neighboring missions with greater frequency, and made longer stays than ever before. Juana began to be anxious, and to wonder what was the cause of these strange proceedings, taking her husband away from her, sometimes for nearly two weeks at a stretch. Questioning Diego was useless, for he was a discreet servant, and told her, simply, that the Father's business called him away. This was far from satisfying her, of course, but she could learn nothing more from him.

Juana, however, was not dependent entirely upon

Diego for information as to what was going on in her little world, that is, at the mission. She was an acute little person in spite of her simplicity, and it would not have taken one as acute as she, to see that something was disturbing the neophytes, and tending to make them unruly. One day, at the hour for shutting up the Indian children for the night, a youth was discovered missing. Search was made, and kept up far into the night and the next day, but without result. Ordinarily this would have excited no great attention, but indications of the troublous times of 1824 had already made their appearance, and every little incident out of the common routine was looked upon with apprehension. The young Indian returned at the close of the next day, and tried to appear as if nothing had occurred. He was taken immediately to the Father, who questioned him long and patiently, but with no avail. He would say nothing farther than that he had run off to the cañon in the mountains for a day's idleness; and this he maintained, while the priest, wearied and harassed, threatened him with flogging.

Juana had heard of this, for news in a little community like the mission flies fast. Several times, when on the way to her work at the mission, either as teacher to the Indian girls, or as spinner and weaver of the fine cloth from which were made the vestments and altar decorations, or, if it chanced to be the Sabbath, to attend mass at the church, she had noticed little groups of the neophytes talking eagerly, but in low voices; but so soon as she approached, they separated and went their several ways, giving her a glance of malevolence, or so it seemed to her, as she passed by. These things were enough to show her that something was stirring the neophytes; and whatever that something was, it meant, in the end, danger to the fathers and to all the Mexicans connected with the mission.

But the most important, and far the most terrifying, indication of something amiss, was the sight Juana had one day while in the cañon near her home. She had taken Pepito with her, and wandered up the cañon to the place where the stream came down the mountainside in a series of little falls, rushing and tumbling among the boulders that filled its path. This was a favorite spot with Juana, and here she came frequently for an afternoon holiday, sitting in the shade of the cottonwood trees lining the brook on either side, working on some piece of embroidery for the church, or, perhaps, some more humble domestic bit of sewing, or, in idle revery, watching the water hurrying by, but never long at a time forgetting her baby, which was always, of course, her companion. On this afternoon Juana had been at her shady nook by the stream, intent on finishing some sewing she had brought with her, before it should come time to go home. Not a sound was heard above the noise of the stream, the crowing of the child lying on the ground, as it plucked the yellow poppies, being lost in the wild rush of the water. Chancing to look up while she was threading her needle, Juana saw an Indian striding rapidly toward the stream, which, reaching its bank, he crossed, springing from stone to stone; climbing the opposite bank, he made his way up the mountainside, and was soon lost to sight behind the brow of a near-by foot-hill. Screened as she was by the deep shade of the trees, the Indian had not seen Juana, and well for her he did not, for her first glance told her he was one of the untamed savages that, at that late day in the efforts made by the missions for their reclamation, were still numerous in various parts of the country. Juana was well enough acquainted with Indian customs to recognise at once that the savage was on some hostile errand. He carried a bow in his hand, together with an arrow ready to use without an instant's loss of time. This might have meant he was on a hunting expedition, had not Juana known there was no game of any kind, excepting jack-rabbits and rattlesnakes, within a radius of several miles from the mission; for the neophytes had, long before, killed everything near. This fact as well as his quick gait, showed her he was not on any peaceful business.

With a prayer of thankfulness in her heart (for there was little doubt the Indian would have killed her, had he seen her) Juana seized her work, and, with the baby in her arms, made all possible haste to her home. Her heart was in her mouth more than once, when she fancied she saw a savage lurking among the trees, or behind some big boulder; but she reached the house without further incident.

Diego, who had been away on one of his long absences, arrived home that same night. When Juana related to him, almost at the first moment of greeting, the incident of the afternoon, Diego listened in surprise and alarm, and when she had finished said:

"Juana, you must not go there again; it is most dangerous. But I do not think you will after what happened to-day. I must go back to the mission, and tell the Father what you saw."

"Tell me, Diego," implored Juana. "I know there is some trouble with the Indians. Is it very serious? Are we all in danger? Remember what they did to Father Jaime at San Diego. But they could not do any harm to the fathers now. We are too strong for them."

"No, Juana," answered Diego, "the fathers are in no personal danger, I think. And the trouble is not here, so much as farther north, at Santa Bárbara, and the missions near there. But the fathers at all the missions are on the watch, for no one knows just where or when the trouble will break forth. The neophytes are dissatisfied, and will not obey their masters. But you must say nothing of this to any one. The Father wishes to keep it as quiet as possible, so as to alarm no one at the mission, and to have none of the Indians think they are suspected. I must go."

And Diego set out for the mission, from whence he did not return until several hours later. The next day saw him off again on one of his long absences, bearing letters from the Father to the priests at Capistrano, San Fernando and the more distant Santa Barbara.

During his absence, Juana hardly dared stir from the house, except to take the beaten road to the mission; and even this required a mustering up of her courage every time she made the short journey, although she knew a foe would be very unlikely to venture into so exposed a position. On the day of Diego's departure, Father Zalvidea had made her relate to him every detail of her episode in the cañon. He feared the worst, but made light of it to her. At the same time he told her she might stay at the mission if she feared to be alone, until such time as the danger should be past. But Juana could not make up her mind to leave her home, her flowers, which she tended so carefully, and her garden, which, without her daily oversight, would be ruined. Thanking the Father, she said she would stay on at home, unless something more should occur.

Day after day went by without further incident of any kind. Indeed, the presence of the Indian in the cañon appeared to be the last of the series of occurrences to cause alarm; and the anxiety of the Father and the Mexicans was quieted. Still, as Diego did not return, they knew that affairs at the other missions were not in an altogether favorable condition.

But at last, after an absence of nearly three weeks, Diego returned, and brought tidings boding no good. There was no trouble apparent impending at San Juan Capistrano, and but little at San Fernando; but at Santa Bárbara, and especially at Santa Inés, to which missions Diego had been sent by the priests at Santa Bárbara, much trouble was feared, and at any moment. The neophytes were watched closely, but there were many gentiles in the mountains around, who had stirred up the mission Indians to a state of great excitement. However, there was nothing to do, except to keep a strict guard.

Juana was overjoyed to see Diego. She had kept on with her daily work at the mission and at home, and, as nothing further had occurred of an alarming nature, she had, by degrees, lost much of her terror. Her anxiety for Diego, too, had helped to draw away her thought from herself and her situation. That was a happy evening for Juana, and her happiness was increased when Diego told her he would not be obliged to leave again for some weeks, unless the outbreak that was feared should materialise to call him away.

Well for us we know not what the morrow may bring forth! Nothing disturbed Juana's happiness that night, and she fell asleep with a sigh of content, and a heart lightened of all fear and anxiety. The next morning Diego went to work in the garden not far from the house, leaving Juana busy with her domestic duties. The day after Diego's return from one of his long absences was always a holiday for Juana, one of the mission women taking her place as teacher. Happy and gay she cleared away the breakfast, swept the room, and washed and dressed the baby, now and then bursting into song, from sheer excess of joy. It was toward the middle of the morning, when she heard a sudden cry from Diego. Springing up, she hastened out of the house, and ran to the spot where she had seen her husband at work a few moments before. It was not until she had reached the place that she discovered Diego, prone on the ground where he had fallen, near the vines he had been pruning. Juana knelt and threw her arms around his neck, when she saw the arrow from which he had fallen, buried deep in his breast.

"Juana, *querida,*" he whispered hoarsely, "get Pepito and fly to the mission. Tell the Father. Leave me; I am past help. The arrow was poisoned. Go at once."

"Diego, Diego, I cannot go; let me die here with you. Let the Indian kill me, too. Where is he?" and she looked wildly around.

"He is hiding among the trees by the stream. Juana, go, I command you. Santa María! Save her from the cruel savage, who may be, even now, watching us."

Enfolding her in a close embrace, he kissed her many times, then, with his remaining strength, pushed her from him and motioned her to go.

Juana did not move. She clung to Diego, weeping bitterly, as she whispered endearing names. The time of delay, however, was not long, for the Indian's aim had been true; and without the aid of the poison with which the arrow was tipped, Diego was doomed. Suddenly Juana felt a tremor pass through him; his head fell back on the ground, and with a deep sigh, he closed his eyes and was dead.

Juana gazed long on the inanimate form of her husband, then, with a last parting kiss, turned toward the house. She thought now of Pepito for the first time since she had left him, and she quickened her steps, going faster as she neared the house, and her fear of the hidden savage came over her. The time she had been absent was short, though it seemed hours to her, and she found the baby playing in the sunlight that streamed in the window. Snatching him up convulsively, she dashed out of the house, and ran at her utmost speed along the road that led to the mission, nearly three miles away. Her horse was tethered in the field, not one hundred yards from her, but she was too frightened to think of that. Her one thought was to get away from the Indian, and to reach the mission, forgetting in her unceasing fear that she was completely at the mercy of her foe, and that, were he bent on still further mischief, by hurrying unduly, she was only hastening the bitter moment.

And so it proved. The road to the mission lay at an acute angle with the course of the stream, and the place where Juana supposed the Indian to be hid was, for some distance, almost in front of her. She hurried on, looking neither to right nor left, but with gaze bent tensely on the mission church, the cross on the roof alone being visible above the tree tops. She had gone only a few yards when she heard a sudden, sharp whistling in the air near her. Startled, she glanced quickly to one side, and clutched the baby more closely to her—too late; she saw not the arrow, such was its velocity, but felt the baby give one spasmodic bound. She flew along the road, the child screaming as she ran. As she neared the mission, and the houses clustered around it, the inmates started from their various occupations and gazed in astonishment at Juana as she sped by, wild-eyed, her hair streaming in the wind.

Father Zalvidea had passed the morning in reading the letters Diego had brought to him the night before, and meditating gloomily on the prospect confronting the missions. He did not fear any particular trouble at San Gabriel, but the news he had had from some of the northern establishments was not reassuring; and the missions were so closely united in one common bond, that what was an injury to one was an injury to all. After reading and re-reading the letters, he put them away, and betook himself to his garden for a little *pasear* before his midday meal. He had paced the length of the garden only two or three times, when he was aroused from his revery by the abrupt appearance of a woman whom, from the agony distorting her face, and her long fluttering hair, he did not at once recognise. As soon as she saw him Juana cried out, "Father, Father!" and staggering forward a step, fell, unconscious, at his feet. Calling loudly for help, the priest bent over, and caught the baby from her arms. At sight of the arrow he exclaimed: "Now may God help us!" for he understood, on the instant, its import.

By this time he was surrounded by a number of women and servants, and, not heeding their ejaculations, he bade them carry Juana into the house. The baby was past help—the arrow had pierced its neck, and the child was even then in the stupor that would give way only to death, the poison working rapidly in the small body. But the Father could not linger. Leaving Juana and the child in care of the household, he quickly alarmed the Mexican contingent of the mission, and put them on guard. A small number of armed men were sent to reconnoitre the mountains near Diego's home. The hunt was kept up for two days; but nothing was found except the tracks of the Indian in the soft mud of the river, and a circle of ashes, the remains of a small fire. From all indications there had been only one Indian in the neighborhood, and he, apparently, had disappeared to return no more, for nothing was seen of him, though a watch was maintained there for several weeks.

Such a state of extreme uncertainty as the mission was in could not have lasted long, and the Father knew that unless something were done to end it, the neophytes would most certainly rise in rebellion, and slay their masters. Fortunately all danger was removed, a few days after Diego's tragic end, by the arrival of a messenger with letters from Santa Bárbara. The news they contained was most grave. The vague, intangible anxiety, so long experienced, had culminated at last in the uprising of the Indians at Mission Purísima. On the Sabbath morning previous, they had made a sudden assault on the mission, and had burned many of the buildings, almost ruined the church, and, after much fighting, had driven the Mexicans with the fathers to Mission Santa Inés, twenty-five miles distant. Word had been sent at once to Monterey, and a detachment of soldiers from the presidio there had hastened to the spot. This required two days, during which the insurgents held the mission; but on the arrival of the troops, they were soon ousted and forced to retire.

The same thing was attempted at Santa Inés, but not much difficulty was found in quelling the disturbance. Some signs of insubordination were shown at the neighboring missions, San Luis Obispo in the north, and Santa Bárbara, San Buenaventura and San Fernando south of the scene of the trouble; but there was no disturbance after the Indians had learned that the attempt at Purísima was unsuccessful; and they hastened to pledge obedience to the fathers. There were four hundred Indians in active insurrection, and although many were wounded, only sixteen were killed.

As for San Gabriel, the shooting of Diego and his child was the only incident that occurred at this mission which showed the condition of things prevailing everywhere; and Father Zalvidea was thankful to have it no worse—yet long he mourned for his faithful servant. When Diego and Pepito were buried, the Father made a solemn and impressive address to the neophytes, painting in vivid colors the pains of hell, which those engaged in the insurrection were in danger of experiencing after death, contrasting it with the joys of those blessed ones who did God's will on earth, and received their own great reward hereafter.

Juana was delirious and raving for many days. The shock itself was sufficient to cause her illness, but it was surmised that the arrow, which had slain Pepito, had entered an inch or so into her arm. In the excitement of her sudden appearance and fainting, when the Father took the child from her, this was not noticed; but a few hours later her arm became much swollen and very painful; and as a slight wound was discovered, the Father concluded some of the poison had entered her system. This was the only plausible theory to account for her swollen arm, and also, perhaps, for her subsequent condition; for Juana, alas! never recovered her mental faculties after the fever left her. Regaining her physical health, the memory of her former life was an almost complete blank. All she seemed to have retained were the refrains of two or three songs she had been accustomed to sing to Diego, in the first months of their married life.

Juana lived for many years, and until she became an old, old woman. She was always treated with the greatest consideration by every one at the mission, for her story was known, at first, as an event in their mission life, then, as the years went by, as history and tradition. Meek and gentle she was. It was only when thwarted in her desires that she became aroused to a pitch of angry insanity which made her dangerous. This chanced very seldom, for she was allowed to do as she pleased in all things. And so she lived, unnoting the many and great changes that took place from year to year in Nueva California—San Gabriel losing its greatness and power, ceasing, even, together with all the others, its life as a mission, and the province itself torn from the grasp of Mexico, to become a member of the greatest republic in the world—her unheeding mind knew nothing of all this. Her favorite pastime, after the railroad was built through the little town of San Gabriel, was to wander down to the station, when time for the trains, which she quickly learned, and to greet them with the snatches of song that remained with her—sole vestige of her former life.

But death came at last to this poor wayfarer on life's journey, and she was buried in the cemetery near the church, by the side of her husband and her child, the place which had been, by common consent, reserved for her in the sadly overcrowded little *campo santo*. Here lies all of her that was mortal. We know she is well once more, with her mind and memory, touched by divine healing, restored to her, and, we may be sure, happy in the companionship of her loved ones.

FATHER URIA'S SAINTS

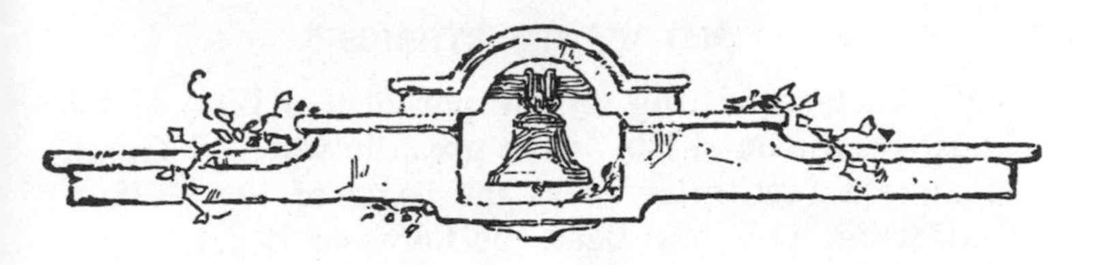

FATHER URIA'S SAINTS

THEREFORE I went to Father Uría and told him your story. He was very kind, and bade me write to you that you might trust him to find you something to do if you should decide to come here. Have no fear; there are not enough men at San Buenaventura to prevent a single man from having all the work he may wish. Make haste and come. Do not delay. Diego."

The reader finished the letter, and there was a silence of some minutes between the two, reader and listener. The former, a young man, not much more than twenty-five years of age, had a moody expression on his dark face. After reading the letter he waited for his companion to speak. But María, his wife, appeared not to notice this, and remained silent.

The two were sitting on the porch of a little adobe house on the outskirts of the presidio town of Tubac, Mexico, a few miles from the coast of the Gulf of California. This had been the home of Benito's parents, and since their death three years before, that of himself and his wife. For a time they had been happy in their hard-working life, for love lightened their toil; but toward the close of the second year in their home they had suffered a series of reverses that sadly crippled Benito's resources. First there had been a season of such heat and drought that all their labor in the dozen acres which Benito cultivated came to naught, and they gathered hardly more than enough to keep them from starving before the next year's harvest. Then one of Benito's horses, of which he had three, and fine ones they were, had been taken sick and died just at the time when it was most needed, during the early summer plowing—both Benito's and his neighbors'; for after the work on his own land was done, Benito worked for others, thus adding something toward their income. The death of his horse was a severe blow to him, not only because he loved his horses, but because his income was greatly curtailed in consequence. With three horses Benito could use a pair every day, and yet allow each horse to rest one day out of three; but with two, it could be done only by losing a day's work out of every three; and this was the plan Benito had followed, for he could not bring himself to use his good steeds every day. This had occurred in the spring following the poor harvest.

Some weeks later, about six months before our story opens, another disaster befell these two unfortunate ones. One night, Benito and María had been awakened by a terrible uproar in their chicken-house. Benito rushed out to find it in flames. Some traveller passing, after smoking a cigarette, had, most likely, carelessly thrown the burning stub among the inflammable boards and loose stuff of the enclosure. Benito did what he could to rescue the hens and chickens, but of all of his flock, he saved a mere score. This last calamity was almost more than María could bear. The hens had been her especial care. She had, under her skillful tending, seen the flock increase from the small nucleus of a dozen, which Benito had bought and given her on her coming to his home, a few days after they were married, to over one hundred. These hens had been the source of no small profit, and by their means Benito was able to put aside a little nest egg each year. And now they must begin again! It was hard, and both felt there was no relief for them. The little they had saved during the first few years had to be used for the summer sowing, and for food until they could gather a harvest. Here, again, Benito found there would not be more than sufficient for their wants, and that, when the next sowing time came, they would be in a worse condition than at present for continuing the struggle for existence. Altogether Benito and María were on the edge of despair.

Shortly after the death of Benito's parents, his elder brother had made one of a band of artisans, laborers and soldiers, in company with two Franciscan priests, to the province of Nueva California. Diego, who was of a roving disposition, had wandered off to the south, working at his trade of carpentry as the mood seized him, or the state of his pocket forced him, now here, now there, until finally he found himself in the coast town of San Blas. This was the point from which many of the expeditions to the northern province set sail; and the busy preparations for departure, which Diego witnessed, fired his desire to join a company about to leave for the remote, half-mythical region in the north. This he did, and, some weeks later, landed at Monterey, whence, in the course of the next year, he worked his way south until he reached Mission San Buenaventura. Here he settled down permanently, having grown tired of his aimless life, and became an active and useful man to the Father. Communication between the two countries in those days was infrequent, and Benito had heard his brother was settled at San Buenaventura only after he had been there nearly a year. Diego described, in glowing terms, the advantages of the province—the fine climate, exceeding fertility of the soil, land to be had for the asking, where everything necessary and desired could be grown, and his own content, far away, though he was, from his old home. This letter had reached Benito when he was at the lowest ebb of his fortunes. The glowing language of his brother's description of Nueva California awakened an intense longing in his heart to go there and make a new beginning under more favorable influences. He said nothing to María, but wrote a letter to Diego, telling of his troubles, and asking if there were room for himself and wife in that new land. This he sent off by a friend to San Blas, where it was given over to a priest who, in turn, was to deliver it into the charge of the next expedition to be sent out. Benito had written nearly six months before, and had about given up looking for an answer, when a neighbor, returning home from the town, handed him a letter as he passed by. His brother gave him encouraging news and advised him to come, ending with the words quoted above. After reading it, Benito hastened to find María, and with her by his side on the little porch he read it again to her.

At last María broke the silence:

"Benito, I am glad you wrote to Diego, and I feel sure the best thing for us to do is to go. How can we keep on in the way we have been doing the last two years? I am tired and disheartened, and I know you are too; but there, in the new land, we could make another start with better courage. Let us go." María looked up at Benito, smiling brightly, but with tears in her eyes.

Benito lost no time in carrying out his plan, and at the end of a few weeks he had sold his house and land, and all his furniture and farming tools, reserving only his horses. These, with a few clothes, and two hundred dollars in gold in his pocket, made up the entire wealth of this poor couple. As Benito wished to keep his horses, he decided to go to the new country overland by way of the Colorado River, and across the desert to Mission San Gabriel. This had been the regular route of the land expeditions of the early days of mission history, and was still used, although less frequently. Benito and María had not long to wait when a company was formed to start out on the long journey of seven hundred miles to Mission San Buenaventura.

At the time of the setting out of our friends in the year 1830, travelling overland from Mexico to California was an easy thing, compared to the hardship and dangers of fifty years earlier. Then, the way, through the desert around the mouth of the Colorado River, was beset by the fierce and powerful Yuma Indians, and unless the band of travellers were large and well armed, it would suffer severely at their hands. But the Yumas had become subdued with time, and travelling made safe. The company with which Benito and María journeyed had no mishap, and after four weeks passed on the way, they arrived, one evening late in October, at Mission San Buenaventura, just as the bells of the mission church were pealing out their evening burden.

What a charming place Mission San Buenaventura was in those days! Situated on the coast, it stood not a half-mile from the water, which it faced, while behind, and close to it, was a line of hills running off into the distance until they disappeared on the horizon. At the time of year our pilgrims first saw it, there was little remaining of the verdant freshness of spring and early summer. But if Nature refuses to permit southern California to wear her mantle of green later than May or June, she has bestowed on her a wealth of warm yellow, red and brown, which, to some, is even more pleasing. The bare ground takes on a vividness of glowing color that is almost incredible, while the hills in the distance run through another gamut of color—from yellow through all the shades of orange to an almost pure pink, with pale blue shadows, changing at sunset to intensest purple. Color is rife in California.

The mission consisted of a large white adobe church, a long line of buildings adjoining in which lived the padre and the Mexicans, and a number of little houses and cabins, some of adobe, but the greater number of straw and rushes, which sheltered the Indians. These little huts were scattered around irregularly on all sides; and to them the inmates were wending their way from their daily toil in the fields and among the horses and cattle, and from all the occupations of a pastoral life. Nothing more beautiful could well be imagined than the picture the mission made in the rosy light of sunset—crowds of savages, children of nature gathered together to receive the rich blessings bestowed on them by the fathers, deriving their authority from the Church whose symbol, the great white building, towering above all else of man's work, stood like a sentinel guarding the religious life of the mission.

Father Uría had been pacing to and fro in front of the mission for more than an hour, waiting impatiently for the expedition from Mexico, which had been expected two days before, its regular time of arrival. It was not at all unusual for these bands to be delayed three or four days, and that without meeting with any accident on the way; but news from home was infrequent to a degree that made an expedition to the province awaited with almost unreasonable impatience. Mail, as well as everything else, came usually by sea; but to send letters by the desert route was by no means rare.

Father Uría was known to all his fraternity in the country for his eccentricity. He was a small, rather stout man, about sixty years of age, every one of which had left its mark upon him; for his had been a life of toil surpassed by but few, even among those self-denying workers in the Lord's vineyard. But the hardships of his life had not quenched his jovial spirits, which were, indeed, irrepressible. A laughing greeting for every one he met, Mexican or Indian, was his habit, one that might have begotten a measure of contempt in the beholder, had the Father not possessed a sternness, latent for the most part, it is true, but which could, on occasion, be evoked to prop up the apparently tottering respect due him. Father Uría was fond, too, of company, not only for its own sake, but because it gave him an excuse for the pleasures of the table, and, in especial, for enjoying the delights of the wine made at Mission San Gabriel, and which was in demand by all the missions. This was a weakness seldom indulged in, for the Father cared not for imbibing this delectable liquid unless assisted by pleasant company; and occasions when this could be had were rare. Let not the reader infer from this that our respected *fraile* was guilty of drinking more than was good or seemly for him. There had been a whisper one time, going the rounds of the missions, that he had been uproariously drunk on some occasion in the past; one slanderous tongue said the priest had been reprimanded by President Sanchez, but we do not believe a word of this. And who would grudge him all the pleasure he might get from the good San Gabriel wine? Think of the poor padre, expatriated for the rest of his days, and in a land that wanted much to make life seem worth the living! Our hearts go out to the Father, as to all the other good men who had done likewise, in deepest sympathy.

It is not our intention to enumerate all the peculiarities of Father Uría. But there was one, before which all the rest sank into insignificance, and that was his excessive fondness for cats. The love of cats is more particularly a feminine trait; and this, together with his strength of mind, marked though it was usually by his geniality, makes it the more surprising in Father Uría's case. Yet such was the fact, and as such was it recognised by all with whom he came in contact; for in this instance it was "love me love my"—cats! This hobby of the friar was one he had had from childhood; but gaining man's estate, he had kept it in subjection (fearing it was not in accord with the strictest propriety, especially after taking orders) until he came to California. Here he had found a life of such loneliness, that, as a refuge from almost unbearable ennui, he had gone back to his youthful feline love with more than youthful ardor. When he came to take charge of the Mission, San Buenaventura, three years before, he had brought with him, carefully watched over, four immense cats, which had long been his pets. These he still had, and in their companionship he found his greatest solace for a life of solitude.

Father Uría continued his walking to and fro, gazing off to the east along the road which the expedition from Mexico must traverse on its way to Monterey. Behind him, almost at his heels, trotted one of his pets, seeming to be perfectly content to follow the footsteps of her master, and showing unbounded joy, when he stopped for a moment to pet and speak to her.

"Well! *gatita mia,* you are the only one to stay with your old master. Where are the others? Off hunting for gophers, I suppose. But here are the travellers at last," and he hurried down the road toward the approaching train, the cat bounding along at his side, or running off every few feet, now this way, now that, to chase a butterfly or mosquito hawk. Once, in her haste to overtake her master, she encountered a horned toad. With a spring to one side, and a loud "spst!" she passed it, for this pet of Father Uría was acquainted with these hated objects, but could never overcome her intense horror of them. We are much afraid this puss is a sad coward.

The Father reached the band of travellers, and he received from the commander the packet of letters destined for the mission. Then, with a few words of welcome to all, he bade them follow him to the mission, where they would find refreshment and shelter for the night. On the way, singling out Benito and Maria (the former from his resemblance to Diego) Father Uría questioned them as to their journey, and plans for their future home at his mission. Benito related his story, and hopes of finding some occupation.

"Diego tells me you are skilled in gardening," said the Father. "Would you like to take charge of my garden and orchard? My gardener is growing too old for work, and I have long had thoughts of retiring him. I have waited only to find some one to take his place, and when Diego told me of you, I thought you might be the one I want. What say you?"

"I thank you heartily, my Father," replied Benito. "I should, indeed, be happy and proud to do that, if I can prove worthy."

They reached the mission, and there Benito found Diego waiting to welcome him. After bidding Benito to come and see him in the morning, as Diego led them away to his own little home, the Father went in, his cat following. Leaving her in the house, the Father passed on to the church, where he performed the usual short evening service of the *rosario,* after which he returned to his habitation. No sooner was he in the house, than he was fairly bombarded by a small army of cats, or so it seemed; for although there were only four, including the one with whom we are already acquainted, one might have thought, from the noise and confusion they made, trying to get at their dear master, that there were a dozen at least.

"Now, my cats, you really must behave yourselves a little better than this," said the Father, with a tone of sternness, which, however, had not the slighest effect, since he began at once to pet them, first one and then another, as they crowded around him. "I know you are hungry, but that is no excuse for making such a disturbance. Come, we shall have supper," and with these words he went into his dining-room, the cats trooping after him.

Father Uría always had his table set with as much variety and luxury as his meagre salary, and the resources of the mission, allowed. He was not a hearty eater, nor, as we have said, did he drink largely of wine, unless he had the support of congenial company, but he insisted on variety. His vegetable garden was his pride, and the object of extremest solicitude. In it he had, in flourishing condition, every sort of edible, including, as well, the fruits especially adapted to that climate. As he was seldom favored with guests, he had made it a custom to have his pet cats bear him company at his meals; and he had trained them so well that they were, in general, as perfectly behaved, in their limited capacity, as the best mannered human being; only occasionally, when hunger gained the upper hand, did they break the bounds of cat-decorum. They had their places opposite the Father, in two chairs, two cats, side by side, in each chair; and there they would sit, looking with meek but hungry eyes, first at the Father, then at the meat and cream destined for their repast.

But it is time these cats were introduced to the reader, for such intimate and (if we may be permitted to use the word) personal friends of the priest should have a regular introduction. Let us begin then, with the first, and, as it happens, the oldest and most sedate one. His name is San Francisco, a solemn-looking beast, large and handsome; he is a maltese, and is admired by all who have seen him. The cat sitting quietly by his side in the same chair is Santa Bárbara, a maltese like her companion, but younger and not so handsome, only because not so large. Next comes, in the second chair, the cat whose acquaintance we have already made, Santa Clara, the Father's usual companion at all times, for she has less roving blood in her veins, and prefers remaining with her master to hunting and other feline diversions. She, too, is maltese, but has white paws, the only deviation from pure blood that any of the four cats show. The last, the youngest and smallest cat (although she can boast of five years of age, and, in any company but the present, would be considered a fine large animal), is Santa Inés, the daughter of Santa Bárbara. She is the one to get into all the mischief of which cats are capable; to run away and lead every one a lively chase until she is found, for the Father (let us whisper it under our breath) would feel nearly as much sorrow at the loss of one of his cats, as he would at losing the soul of one of his neophytes.

We fear much that our reader will be ready to set Father Uría down as a mere fool, or a half-crazy old man, and to sneer at him and his precious cats. But are not we all crazy on some subject; has not each one of us some hobby or idiosyncrasy which makes us appear more or less demented to our neighbors? And just because the twist in our poor Father's mind takes the particular form of a love for cats, why should we, how dare we, say he is crazy? No, he was no more crazy than are we; and perhaps his beautiful cats kept him from becoming so, in very sooth, forced to live in the wilderness, if we may call it that, deprived of all the happiness of his native land, and of the friends for whom these cats make a poor substitute at the best.

But there is one point on which we cannot find excuse for the Father, that is, in giving his cats the names of some of the most respected and venerated saints among the Franciscans; going so far, indeed, as to bestow upon his finest cat the name of Saint Francis himself, the founder of the order. It is difficult to conceive of such irreverence in a priest, himself a member of that great order in the Catholic Church; and it is this, if anything, which would show a weakness of the mind. But even here, let us say, not as excuse, but in mitigation of his offence, that only from inadvertence did the Father speak to, or of, his cats by these names in any one's hearing; and there were only two or three people at the mission who knew after what august personages they were called. Besides, their full title was usually reserved for occasions of reprimand, and with these well-mannered creatures such occasions were rare indeed.

"Well," said the Father, beginning his own supper,

after having given the cats each their portion of meat in a large, deep plate, flanked by a saucer brimming full of sweet cream, "aren't you pretty cats to go off and leave me the whole afternoon? Clara was the only one to keep me company. What is the use in having four cats to amuse me, if you mean to run off whenever the notion seizes you? I want you cats to be home all the time. You, San Francisco, should have stayed here with Clara as you are the largest. I think I shall have to tie you up to-morrow. No, I believe I'll punish you now by taking away your supper," saying which, the Father reached across the table and removed the plate of meat and the cream from in front of Francisco, who had just begun to devour his repast. "Miou! Miou!" said Francisco, piteously, looking after his supper, which the priest put down on the table near his own. It was too much: Francisco forgot his manners and with one bound he leaped across the table, snatched up a piece of meat, and, with a growl of defiance, began chewing it vigorously. The Father laughed and returned the cat's supper. "I am afraid, Francisco, you did not catch much in your hunt this afternoon, for you appear to be as hungry as usual. So I won't punish you by depriving you of your supper. Go back to your place."

After supper, the Father, accompanied by his friends, made a tour of the mission to see that everything was safe for the night; then, returning to his house by the church, he spent the evening reading the letters and messages brought to him that day, and in studying for an hour or so by the help of the few theological books his library boasted. Father Uría was an intelligent and well-educated man, and took delight in the investigation of the abstruse subjects and doctrines his Church afforded. He did this from natural inclination, and not from any practical use to be made of such study in his capacity as head of the mission. People in Nueva California, in those days, not only the Indians, but the Mexicans and Spaniards, were of the utmost simplicity of mind, entirely unable to grasp anything beyond the rudiments of their faith.

Early the next morning Benito made his appearance. The Father conducted him out to his garden, and showed him the method he had pursued in bringing everything to a high state of cultivation. Irrigation was not absolutely essential, as at many of the other missions; but, notwithstanding, Father Uría had evolved a miniature system in his garden by means of a spring in the foot-hills, half a mile away, from which water was brought in a narrow flume. This had long been in use for the general needs of the mission; but it was reserved for Father Uría to apply some of the surplus water to the garden. Father Uría had once visited the garden at Mission San Gabriel which had been the special pride and comfort of Father Zalvidea; and it was with complacent satisfaction that, in comparing it with his own, he saw the latter suffered no disparagement. His was in fully as flourishing condition, but the element of picturesque beauty was lacking; his needs for a garden were entirely utilitarian, while Father Zalvidea required beauty quite as much as use. The two gardens were typical of the two men. So Benito was installed as his gardener.

While the Father was showing Benito the garden, and explaining to him about the plants, the cats which, as usual, had followed him, employed the time in roaming around among the bushes, searching intently for anything alive which might make fair game. They scattered in all directions, one after a humming-bird, another chasing a butterfly; the third wandered off lazily to a big patch of catnip for a sniff of its delightful aroma; while the fourth began to career to and fro after a dragon-fly, in the wildest fashion. The priest and Benito had moved off to an asparagus bed, to consult about the best treatment to give it, for the plants were slowly dying, and the Father was in a quandary. The dragon-fly alighted to rest on his broad-brimmed hat. All unconscious of its presence, he talked on with Benito, expounding his theory of the proper treatment for the asparagus, when, suddenly, as he bent over a plant to look at it more closely, with a blow that almost knocked him down, his hat went flying from his head, and fell to the ground several yards away, while at his feet dropped the venturesome Inés. She was up in an instant, looking for her prey, but it was out of sight.

With an exclamation rather stronger than was quite proper in one of his cloth, the Father turned to the cat.

"What is the meaning of this business, Inés? Really, you are getting to be insufferable. I cannot allow you to come out with me if you carry on in this way." Benito had run to pick up his hat, and offered it to him, his eyes dancing with merriment, and the corners of his mouth twitching. The Father took it, and noting the gleam in his eyes, smiled himself. "These cats of mine will be the death of me some day, I expect," he said, laughing. "Go along, Inés, and remember to show a little more respect for your master another time."

These saints of Father Uría were given the run of the entire mission, and were known to all its inhabitants. Although every one was kind to them, the cats were dignified and distant toward all but the Father and Benito, after the latter had lived there a few months. It had gradually become one of Benito's duties to keep an eye on them; shut them up when the Father did not wish them around; and when, as occasionally happened, they ran away, to search for them. Usually they would return of their own accord the second day, if not found the night before; but the Father could not sleep unless he knew his precious animals were housed safely, and an effort was always made to find the truants before night set in.

From the time Benito and María made San Buenaventura their home, Fortune again turned her face toward them. Benito, with steady employment as the Father's gardener and trusted servant, was prosperous and happy; while María once more had her chickens, although the demand for her poultry and eggs was smaller than she had found in her former home in Mexico. She seldom missed her old associates, busy as she was, and content with her simple tasks the whole day long. What a quiet, peaceful life was that at the California missions in the old days! Perhaps, reader, you think humdrum would be the more appropriate adjective to use than peaceful or even quiet. And to one like our Father Uría, thousands of miles from his early home, cut off from all the pleasures and advantages of ordinary social intercourse, it was, as we have seen, more, much more, than humdrum. But for María, the life at the mission was not unlike that they had been accustomed to in their former Mexican home. California was Mexico in those days, and the life greatly similar.

About two years after Benito's arrival at San Buenaventura, a dreadful misfortune befell Father Uría, in the death of his largest and finest cat—San Francisco. This saint had always manifested a most singular and inveterate propensity to hunt tarantulas. More than once he had been discovered when just on the point of beginning a battle with one of those monsters, and had been stopped in the nick of time. With almost constant watchfulness, the Father had succeeded in preserving the life of his cat for many years; but the reader has already guessed what the end was to be. After an absence of three whole days, during which the Father was almost distracted, Benito found the saint dead on the plain, fully a mile from the mission. On one paw, which was slightly swollen, a minute wound was discovered, supposed to have been the bite of the venomous spider, although the Father could not tell positively. Poor Father Uría was inconsolable, and from that day his health, which had been deserting him for many months, yet so gradually as to be hardly perceptible, took a sudden change for the worse, and with the long years of toil he had lived, soon made great inroads on his strength. Less than a year after this dire event, he became so feeble that, at his own request, he was relieved. The last thing he did before leaving San Buenaventura was to give his three remaining friends into the charge of Benito, who promised to care for them faithfully so long as they lived. Much the Father would have liked to take them with him, but he was growing too feeble to care for them; and once retired from his position as head of the mission, he would not have enough power and authority to be able to treat them as such old and dear friends should be treated. We shall not attempt to depict the sorrowful parting between the Father and his cats—it would need the master hand of a Dickens to keep the comic element in the pathetic scene within due bounds. The Father, poor old man, felt no further interest in life, broken down in health and obliged to give up his companions, his only comfort being the thought that his remaining days were few, and would soon pass.

He removed to Mission Santa Bárbara, and there, some months later, at the close of the year 1834, he died, worn out in the cause of his Master.

NOTE.—This story of Father Uría and his oddities is not wholly fanciful. In an early book on California occurs the following: "At dinner the fare was sumptuous, and I was much amused at the eccentricities of the old Padre [Father Uría], who kept constantly annoying four large cats, his daily companions; or with a long stick thumped upon the heads of his Indian boys, and seemed delighted thus to gratify his singular propensities." Alfred Robinson: *Life in California,* New York, 1846, Chap. IV, page 50.

POMPONIO

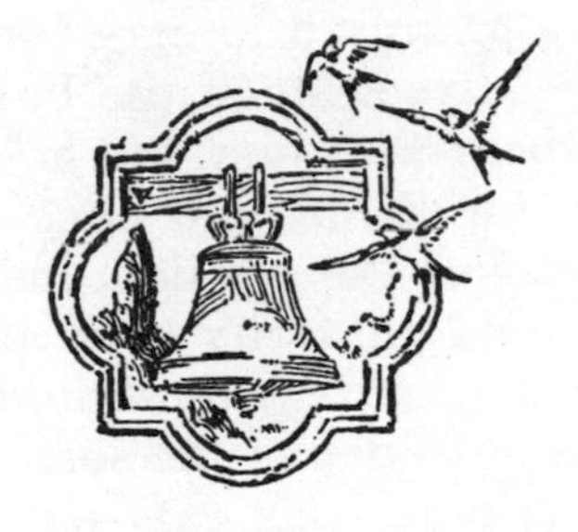

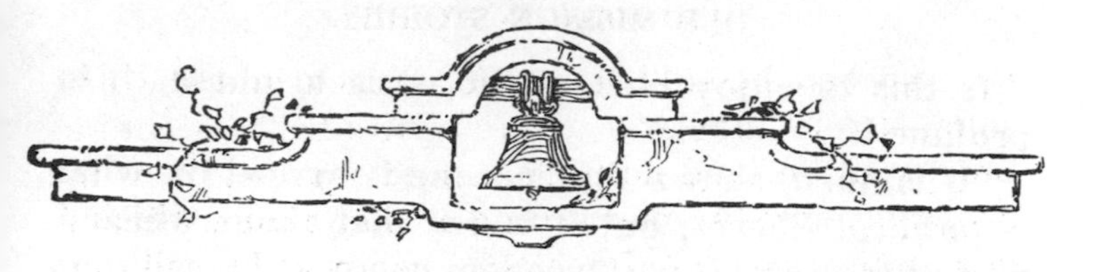

POMPONIO

LIBERTY! Liberty! For a half-century we have done nothing but repeat this word, and one would say that those mouths which pronounce it belong to the heads which are ignorant of its meaning, or rather that it has no meaning; for, if one says: 'We are free!' ten others cry out at once: 'We, we are oppressed!' Such an one who found, a few years ago, too great a freedom, to-day demands very much more; and this is, doubtless, because each one has his own idea of liberty, and it is impossible to create a liberty for each one.—Liberty to empty the treasury of the state.—Liberty to seize public position.—Liberty to gather in sinecures.—Liberty to get one's self pensioned for imaginary services.—Liberty to calumniate, abuse, revile the most venerated things.

—Is this to enjoy liberty? No, it is to abuse it, to profane it.

"It is, then, shown that no one is agreed on what is political liberty; but it is not that about which I wished to write. It is a freedom composed, I will not say of all men, but of all beings who are in existence; it is this that nature demands imperiously; it is this, in truth, that crime compels society to take away from the wrong-doer; but it is this, also, that injustice and force snatch away from the unhappy slave."

Thus wrote Captain Duhaut-Cilly in his journal for the year 1827, contrasting his ideal of freedom with the actual condition of the aborigines in California, under the domination, as they were at that time, of the Catholic Church, through its agent, the order of the Franciscans.

Just a few words are necessary here as an introduction to the story of Pomponio, to enable the reader to have a clear impression of the condition of affairs, political and ecclesiastical, in the province of Nueva California during the first thirty years of the past century. When the country was explored and settled by the Franciscans, their ostensible and, in the earlier days, real, aim was to civilise the Indians, teaching them to live useful, moral lives, and instructing them in the doctrines of Christianity. But to do this, force was necessary to subdue the turbulence of insubordination. Gradually, at last, the greater number of the natives were forced under the rule of the friars, who brought them to such subjection as was actual slavery in all but in name. It is a matter of regret that this was so, yet, though an evil, it was a necessary one, for to do any measure of good to the Indians, an oversight in every detail was essential; and, after all, the savages were treated with almost uniform mildness, and the instances of cruelty and wickedness practised toward them, as in this tale of Pomponio, were most happily very rare. It is a blot on the history of the Franciscans in California that there was a single instance of anything but kindness and humanity; but the truth cannot be ignored, however much it grieve us to know it. Let us turn to Pomponio. His is a strange tale.

Distant about a league south from Mission San Francisco stood a little Indian hut, made from the tules and rushes which were found growing with such luxuriance in all parts of Nueva California. It was built in the form of a cone with a blunt apex, was less than ten feet in diameter, and but little more than that in height. An opening near the ground gave communication with the outer air, and a small hole at the top of the hut allowed the smoke from the fire to pass away. This hut stood in the centre of a small open spot among the trees of the dense forest which surrounded it on all sides; small in extent like the many other wooded spots in the peninsula which terminated at the mission and the presidio of San Francisco, but sufficiently large to force a stranger to them to lose his way almost at the first step. But, difficult to find by the stranger, this little open space was correspondingly safe from pursuit by any one bent on hostile deeds; and for this reason it had been selected by Pomponio for a retreat for himself.

Pomponio was a mission Indian, had been connected with the religious establishment since boyhood, and had made great progress on the way to becoming a civilised human being. He had a mind above the low level of the average Californian Indian intellect, and had been an object of solicitude to the padres, arousing in them an interest in his mental and spiritual welfare seldom evoked by the neophytes in general. For years Pomponio had been contented with the life he led under the tutelage and control of the fathers, receiving unquestioningly their teaching, and regarding their ordering and direction of his and his parents' life and actions in every particular with indifferent eyes. But when Pomponio left childhood and youth behind him, and acquired the mind of a man, Indian though it was, he began to see the state of things in a different light. "What right have these padres," he would say to himself, "to come here from far away, take our land from us, make us work for them, and order us about as we should women and children taken from our enemies in war? And what do they give us in return? They teach us the religion of their God, and make us learn their catechism. Is their religion any better than ours, their God more powerful than the Great Spirit? What better is it to till the ground for growing food than to kill the wild animals with bow and arrow? Why did my father's father and all the strong men of those days permit these *españoles* to come here? I would have withstood them to the last drop of my life's blood."

Thus would Pomponio question. The Indians of Nueva California were mild and gentle, having nothing in common with their neighbors, the warlike Yumas, and were easily subjected by the early Franciscans. But gentle and pliant as they were, there were always a few, fiercer than the rest, who did not brook calmly the sight of their subjection; and these bolder ones stirred up, from time to time, the other natives to insurrection. Many were the uprisings at the different missions—one of the earliest at San Diego, in 1775, when the savages killed one of the padres; one, the last, and only a few months before the beginning of our tale, late in 1824, when the two missions, Purísima and Santa Inés, were almost destroyed. This last uprising had had more to do with Pomponio's change of attitude toward the fathers than anything else; and it had fired his zeal to devote his life to the freeing of his kindred and tribe from the slavery in which they were held at Mission San Francisco.

Pomponio, simple savage that he was, knew little of human nature, either Indian or civilised. He judged others by himself, not realising the great difference between himself and the generality of the tribe to which he belonged. He had had many talks with the various men of the tribe, trying to instill into their minds some of the ferment of his own; but to his amazement and anger they were too far sunk in their servitude to be roused by his projects. A few there were, young and venturesome like himself, who declared themselves ready to follow him as a leader; and among these were some of the fierce savages of the forests, with whom he was always in touch; but how could a mere handful of a score of Indians cope successfully with the men of the mission, aided, as they would be, by the trained soldiers of the presidio? Pomponio had sense enough to see that such procedure would be foolhardy, and he abandoned the plan for the time, hoping his little body of followers would increase, when the disparity in strength and numbers between the two sides might be less.

Pomponio was some twenty-three years old. A short time before he had married an Indian girl, and, with her, lived in a little adobe house, a few paces from the mission church. Pomponio and Rosa had lived the regular life of the neophytes, working at various occupations of the community—Pomponio tilling the ground and caring for the crops, and helping in the making of bricks for the houses; Rosa spinning and weaving and cooking. After they were married they continued with their customary labors, still under the tutelage of the fathers. But about this time Father Altimira had begun to notice the alteration in Pomponio's demeanor. Wondering at the change in one of his most promising neophytes, he had sought to find a clue to the mystery. From an unquestioning readiness in everything pertaining to his mission life, Pomponio had begun to neglect his duties, shirking the tasks given him, wandering off among the mountains and stirring up the mission Indians to a state of dissatisfaction and ill-feeling. Father Altimira had seen Pomponio's growing negligence with concern, but to his questioning Pomponio would give no answer as to the reason for his new attitude toward his masters. The Father, finding that persuasion was of no avail in correcting Pomponio's disobedience, had him locked up in the mission prison for twenty-four hours, after which he was released with a reprimand and warning.

Pomponio walked out of the prison and to his house without a word. For a few days he was quiet and attentive to his work, not from fear of the consequences of doing otherwise (that is not the Indian nature, even of those poor natives of Nueva California), but because he was awaiting his opportunity for inflicting some injury on his persecutors, as he had come to think of them.

One night Father Altimira, who was a light sleeper, awoke, thinking he had heard a faint noise in the room adjoining his bed-room, which was used as a store-room for the books, the rich vestments embroidered with gold and silver threads, and the money belonging to the mission. At this time there was, in the strong iron-bound chest used for the safekeeping of these valuables, a sum of nearly five thousand dollars in gold, and the Father's first thought on waking, was of this money. Rising on his elbow, he listened. Hearing nothing, he was about to lie down, when again came the sound which had disturbed him, scarcely louder than the chirp of a far-away cricket, and which, but for the utter silence of the night, would have been swallowed up in the thick depths of the adobe wall between the two rooms. Springing out of bed, he threw on his clothes, and without a thought of danger to himself, hurried out to the cloisters and the next room. The night was dark, and he could not make out anything until he reached the window of the room from which came the noise. The heavy wooden shutters were slightly ajar, and through the narrow upright opening between them, filtered the faint light from a small lantern in the room. With noiseless steps, Father Altimira approached the window, and looked through the crack between the two shutters. There, in front of the iron-bound box, knelt Pomponio, busily at work on the stout padlock that guarded the treasures within. With all the strength of his powerful arms he filed away at the bar of the padlock. For a moment the Father forgot his part in the nocturnal business, and stood, breathless, at the window, fascinated by the quick motion of the arm back and forth, and the strident sound of the file as it slowly ate its way through the steel. Suddenly Pomponio paused and looked up, with an expression of fear and hate on his face, dreadful to see. Snatching up the lantern from the floor, he dropped it behind the great box, and ran to the window. The Father stooped, and crouched close against the wall under the window—for there had not been time to get away—and waited, hardly daring to breathe. Pomponio carefully opened the shutters and peered out, but he could distinguish nothing in the intense blackness. After listening a moment and hearing no sound, he closed the shutters and went back to his work. The priest waited until he again heard the screech of the file before he dared to move. This action of Pomponio recalled him to himself, and the responsibility resting on him regarding the safety of the mission funds.

With hasty strides, the Father started off to seek assistance. He hurried to the other end of the row of buildings, some three hundred feet distant, where lived the Mexican servants of the mission. At the house of the carpenter, which was the first he came to, the priest rapped loudly on the door, and called to the occupant to awaken. Juan, the carpenter, answered almost at once, and came to the door. Before he could ejaculate a word of surprise on seeing the Father, the latter had told him the trouble.

"Arouse, with all haste, the men in the next house, while I go for Rafael. Be ready when I come back," and the Father hurried off.

Juan lost no time in awakening the two men in the house near-by. A moment after, the Father returned with Rafael, the overseer, and together the five men ran swiftly and silently to the scene of the disturbance. Nearing the window through which Pomponio had forced an entrance, the carpenter stepped up to it softly. The Father's absence had not been longer than five minutes, and the thief was still hard at work filing the padlock. Muttering to Rafael to follow him, and the other two men to guard the window without, Juan noiselessly pushed open the heavy shutters, and sprang through the window, Rafael close at his heels.

It was not until both men had passed through the

window, so quick were their movements, that Pomponio became aware he was discovered. Looking up, he dropped the file, snatched up the lantern and hurled it against the wall, shivering it into pieces. Just as the light went out the men seized him. Pomponio fought like a demon, and was fast getting loose from their clutches, when Juan shouted to the men outside to come to their aid; but too late. As they clambered through the window, and sought to lay hold of him, which was not the work of a moment in the darkness, the neophyte broke from his antagonists and sprang to one side, avoiding the oncoming couple from the window. While the men were shouting and swearing, groping this way and that to find their prey, Pomponio slid softly to the window, jumped through it, and set off, at his utmost speed, for the open plain and not far distant forest. During the fray Father Altimira had remained somewhat apart, outside the room. As Pomponio rushed by him, the Father, calling him by name, commanded him to stop. He paid no attention, but kept on his way, and was immediately lost in the darkness. By this time the four men had piled out of the window, falling over each other in their eagerness to pursue the fast escaping game.

"It is useless to follow him," cried the Father. "You could not find him in this gloom. Wait till daylight, and we will hunt for him. We must see what damage he has done in the store-room. Stay here. I will get a light."

The Father went to his chamber, and brought out

a lighted lantern, and with this the men returned to the now quiet room, entering by the door which the priest unlocked with the key he had taken from its hiding place in his own room. With the exception of the shattered lantern, and the file and hammer lying on the floor, everything was in order. The bar of the padlock was almost filed through—three minutes more, and Pomponio would have been away with his booty. As further sleep that night was out of the question, the Father and one of the men remained on guard in the room until dawn, the others reconnoitring every half-hour to see that all was quiet around the mission.

When morning came, the first thing the Father did was to send a messenger to the presidio, four miles distant, with a letter to the commandant, relating the occurrence of the night, and asking for a guard for the mission, and a number of men to take up the hunt for the escaped culprit. The soldiers arrived during the day, and at once made active preparations for finding Pomponio. Beyond knowing the general direction he had taken in fleeing from the mission, which the padre had noted as well as he could in the darkness, the hunters were wholly at sea as to where to look. He might be in any part of the hills and forests which surrounded the mission on all sides. To the north he would probably not go, for that way lay the presidio, and the country was more open and travelled, as well as terminating, at no great distance, at the water's edge of the bay. It would be difficult, if not impossible, to find an Indian of Pomponio's intelligence, but the soldiers began their task, searching near and far, visiting the various *rancherias* and the wild remnants of the natives. They scoured the country for many days, but without result. We shall leave them for a while, and see what is become of our fugitive.

As Pomponio passed the Father in his flight from the room, to rob which he had made such a bold and nearly successful attempt, he heard the priest calling him to stop; but what cared he for his master? Had not he been fleeing for his liberty and, perhaps, for his life, he would have killed the Father on the spot: not because he hated his kind teacher, but because in him was embodied the life of the mission, or so it seemed to Pomponio; and his death would have been one blow given toward the freedom of his kind. But Pomponio's first thought now was for his own safety, and he took the shortest course to the forests south of the mission. As much at home among the great trees as at the mission, he made his way into their depths with unerring aim, in spite of the Egyptian darkness, until he reached a slight thinning of the trees, where he halted. The spot, mentioned at the beginning of this tale, was a favorite of Pomponio, and one he visited from time to time, when he wished to be free to hold communication with the wild men in the neighborhood. Here he felt reasonably secure from surprise, and here he meant to spend the days to come.

There was an old Indian hut in the open space which once had sheltered some family, and was now abandoned. Pomponio took possession of this. When daylight came, he went in search of the savages in the forest, and on finding them, he recounted his adventure and the consequences to himself. Among the Indians were the larger number of those who had sworn allegiance to Pomponio, promising to follow him whenever he should decide for a general extermination of the detested Spaniards. They welcomed him warmly, and supplied him with food and everything he needed for his hut. The Indians not included in his band of followers had, heretofore, looked askance on Pomponio, and had sought to withdraw him from the mission into their own wild life. This he had refused to do, contending, with more than usual Indian intelligence, that he would be able to wreak greater harm to the Spanish if connected with the mission. This had been the principal reason for his small following. Now that he had broken definitely with his old life, they espoused his cause almost to a man, and at last he had the joy of seeing himself at the head of a very respectable band of nearly fifty determined men. The majority of them were for advancing to the enemy without a day's delay, and striking a decisive blow once for all. But Pomponio refused.

"No," he said. "Wait until the excitement of last night dies away; then we shall stand a better chance of winning. But now the mission will be on guard, and we should be defeated."

This cogent reasoning prevailed, but the hotheaded youths grumbled much and long at the delay.

Pomponio, himself, chafed at their enforced inaction, necessary though he knew it to be. Then another thing that troubled him was the thought of his wife. Would they think she knew of his attempt that night, and punish her? He had told her nothing, but whether she could make the Father believe it, was another matter. Much he wished he could have some communication with her, and tell her where he was, and beg her to join him. But it was too dangerous. Without a doubt she was watched closely, if she were not actually imprisoned. So he gave up all thought of it.

The days dragged slowly along for Pomponio and his companions. Several times during the following two weeks he heard reports of the doings of the mission from different ones of the Indians who went thither to reconnoitre. From these he learned that the soldiers were still kept there, and while they remained on guard, nothing could be done. Once Pomponio stole up to the more distant houses of the mission in the gathering dusk of approaching night. He heard the chant of the fathers and their servants at their evening devotions. All was calm and quiet, and he was just about to risk the attempt to go to his old home, in the hope of seeing Rosa, when a soldier came into view from behind the church. Pomponio crouched down behind a shrub near which he was standing, and waited until the man disappeared again from sight in his round of the buildings. Then noiselessly he crawled away to his companions in the forest.

It was about two weeks after Pomponio's flight.

He had been holding a council of war with his followers, and had told them that, at last, the time was come to strike for liberty. The soldiers at the mission had not been seen for some days, and it was thought they had returned to the presidio. What a shout of exultation went up from the Indians! Now the time was at hand, the time they had looked forward to for so long, when, at one single blow, they hoped to free themselves from their hated oppressors. Vain hope! Had they forgotten already what was the fate of a similar uprising in the southern missions only a few months before? But each one learns from his own experience. The Indian is sanguine, and hopes to succeed where others have failed, or carries out his purposes, desperately and without hope, to end in certain failure. This is not an Indian trait exclusively; it is a question of the weak overpowered by the strong, and has shown itself in all parts of the earth and in every race of mankind. See how well treated were the Indians of Nueva California by their conquerors, mild, humane and devoted to their interests, having given up home and friends to isolate themselves in a wild new country, solely to bestow on these gentiles the blessings of civilisation and, above all, the gift of Christ's religion. We may wonder why they were not willing and glad to follow the fathers', almost without exception, gentle guidance. But the one thing necessary to make it a complete success was wanting—freedom. That was the keystone on which all depended: lacking that, the whole mission system was, by just so much, a failure.

Pomponio was returning to his hut late that day after telling his followers to hold themselves in readiness for marching on to the mission on the nightfall of the morrow. He had nearly reached his habitation, and was walking slowly and with downcast head, buried deep in thought over the approaching conflict which he had wished for so long. Pomponio saw clearly that the task before him and his band was a difficult one. He was not blind to the fact that, even should they succeed at this mission, there would be left in the land twenty others, each one of which would give aid in quelling a revolt at San Francisco, and punishing the insurgents. But Pomponio was in a desperate mood. He preferred failure and death to his life at the mission, and he knew his present life as a fugitive could not last; he would certainly be captured sooner or later.

He walked slowly on. Had not he been so absorbed in thought of the crisis of his life, on the brink of which he stood, the indications of something unusual and foreboding would have arrested his attention. A rustling among the leaves and brush of the undergrowth told of the presence of some animated thing, human or brute. Once a gleam, as of some highly burnished metal flashing in the sun, was to be detected—that surely was no animal! But Pomponio walked on oblivious to these signs which, at any other time, he would have been the first to notice. He was within a few yards of the hut, and on the edge of the clearing, when he heard a crackling among the branches under-foot, and a rushing toward him. One glance was enough. Three soldiers, armed with muskets, were upon him, one on each side, the third in front. They were close to him before he was aware of their presence, and escape was impossible, for he was seized and his arms bound behind him almost as soon as he knew he was captured.

"Aha! we have you at last," cried the leader. "You thought we could not find you out here, hiding in the forest. And I must say it has been hard enough and taken long enough. But we have you safe now, you rascal."

Pomponio said not a word. From the first, so soon as he saw he was helpless, he submitted quietly, and suffered the soldiers to bind his arms with the leathern thong they had brought with them. Had his Indian followers been within sound of his voice, he would have shouted to them to come, not to rescue him—that could not have been done, for the soldiers, at the instant of his call and the answering cries of the Indians, would have shot him dead—but to kill the soldiers. The Indians were too far distant for this. How the soldiers had escaped the savages was a mystery. They must have been at his hut soon after his leaving it that morning, and kept watch for the return of its inmate, thinking it might be Pomponio himself, or some one who would lead to the discovery of his whereabouts. Only in this way could they have missed the Indians roaming in the forest that day, as they made their preparations for the eventful morrow.

"Now, my man, off to the presidio," said the leader,

after they had finished binding Pomponio's arms securely. "We have no time to lose; the sun is low in the west, and will be set long before we get there. So step lively all."

The soldiers picked up their muskets, and started off quickly in the direction of the mission, Pomponio guarded by a man on each side, grasping his pinioned arms. Alas! Was this the end of his long, long planning; was this the outcome of the insurrection which was to have been the prelude to a glorious victory, that he should have been caught through his own carelessness and carried off ignominiously to prison? Pomponio could have sacrificed his life gladly for the cause he had so much at heart; but to be captured before the blow for liberty had been struck was unbearable. He had been the prime mover in planning the revolt, and well he knew his capture sounded the knell, for no one could take his place successfully as leader.

The soldiers hurried their prisoner forward almost on the run, partly because it was so late, and they had a long walk before them, partly from fear of encountering some of the savages they knew were in the forest. However, they were not molested, and reached the mission, lying on their way, as the last bit of sunset color faded away on the horizon. They delayed only long enough to relate the circumstance of the capture, and to get two of the soldiers, acting as guard at the mission, to accompany them to the presidio. Pomponio did not see the Father, who was engaged with the sick in the hospital, and he was glad. After a stop of a few minutes, they again took up their march, and reached the presidio a little later. Here the commandant of the garrison, after having heard the tale of the leader, and taken a look at Pomponio, ordered him to be chained to the wall in a room of the prison. This was done. The chains were fastened around his ankles; his arms were unbound, and he was left to solitude and darkness.

Poor savage captive! Alone, abandoned, and chained to the wall of the little cell he was in, so closely that he could barely reach the low, rough bench on which to sit. But Pomponio could have borne his imprisonment patiently, even cheerfully, had the rebellion only taken place, successfully or not. That was the maddening thought. He buried his head in his hands. Well he knew that all hope was over. Even though he might manage to escape, he would find the Indians dispersed and in hiding, too frightened at the effect his capture might have on the Spaniards, and the result to themselves. All was over. He had nothing farther to live for. Even the thought of Rosa failed to rouse him, for he knew he had been too wicked in the eyes of the fathers to be permitted to see her again—whether in prison or liberated, if such a thing could have been dreamed of, she was dead to him.

Yet the love of life is implanted too deeply in the human breast to die before life itself deserts our mortal body. As Pomponio crouched there, bound and forsaken, a passionate feeling of revolt at his doom arose within him. Was he to be killed; must he leave this earth, beautiful to him even when in the lowest depths of misery, and that, too, at the command of his enemies, who had stolen his country and made him and his kindred slaves? They *should* not take his life, the only thing they had left him. And with the wish came into his mind a plan of escape that made him start.

When the soldiers arrested and imprisoned Pomponio, they neglected to search him, thinking, no doubt, that by no possible means could he escape from them, chained as securely as if to the solid rock itself. Pomponio had, stuck in his belt underneath his shirt, a hunting-knife, his trusty weapon and constant companion. No one who has not lived in the wilderness can have any idea of the value of the hunting-knife. The uses to which it can be put are countless. It is pocket-knife, scissors, hatchet, dagger, and all cutting and stabbing instruments in one; it will, moreover, take the place of revolver and rifle on many occasions, and has one immense advantage over them—its utter silence. It is a powerful, and, at need, murderous weapon.

Pomponio pulled out his knife from its leather sheath and examined it by touch, for it was too dark to see it. He felt carefully of the blade; yes, it was sharp as a razor, and would do the work wanted of it. He grasped it nervously, but firmly, in his right hand. Then he paused. Was it, after all, worth the pain he must suffer; had life anything in store for him in recompense for what he must endure? He could not expect to be again a power among his brethren. At the best he would be the mere wreck of what he had, till now, been to his followers. They might look to him for counsel and advice: as a leader he could be of no more use. Again, admitting he had the courage to do the deed, could his strength hold out until he reached a place of safety? Suppose he fell helpless on the way; he would be found and brought back. Yet to do nothing was to receive certain death, or what, to Pomponio, with his Indian pride, was worse, a public whipping, such as he had heard was given sometimes for grave offences; and afterward such humiliation in his life of bondage as was not to be borne. No, anything to free himself out of the hands of his persecutors. He hesitated no longer.

Clutching the knife, he stooped. Taking firm hold of his foot, as it rested on the ground, with his left hand, he poised the edge of the knife on his heel, back of the iron ring; then, with all his strength, he gave one quick, sharp cut downward and severed the prominence of the heel, removing the greater part of the *os calcis*. Not a sound passed his lips. Letting fall the knife, he pushed the ring down over the wound and the length of his foot. One foot was free, but only one; he was still as much a prisoner as before. Could he bear the torture again?

He gave himself no time to think, but picking up the knife, repeated, with convulsive strength, the operation on his other foot. With a low moan, wrung from him by the double agony, he leaned, faint and deathly sick, against the wall. In this position he remained for many minutes, until, above the pain, arose the thought that he was not yet free.

The small window of the prison was within easy reach from the floor, and it would have been the work of an instant to vault through it, had Pomponio not been disabled by the ugly wounds he had inflicted upon himself. With a sigh he stood up slowly on his maimed feet. Think of the power of will of the poor Indian, his love of life, and, more than his love of life, his hatred of his oppressors, to go through the agony each movement caused him! He crept up to the window, laid hold of the sill, and, with his hands, drew himself up to, and through it, the blood spouting from his wounds at every inch of progress. Lowering himself from the window, he lay down on the ground to gather a little strength for flight. But first he must bind up his feet, in order that his blood might not betray whither he went. Taking off his cotton shirt, he tore it in half, and wrapped each foot in a piece. The touch of the cloth to his wounds was like fire; but by this time his nerves were benumbed to such a degree that he scarcely noticed it.

Going on hands and knees, he started to creep over the distance lying between him and the fringe of trees near the presidio. There was a good half-mile, and Pomponio feared he could not cover it. Four times he fell to the ground unconscious, four times he revived and pushed on with all the strength he could muster. Fortunately he had started early in the night, for he needed every minute of the darkness.

Foot after foot, yard after yard, he crept along, the presidio and the other buildings receding in the increasing distance behind him, while the welcome woods and hills, his refuge, loomed up, higher and darker, as he neared them. At last he reached the shelter of the trees, his friends, as the first faint streaks of the dawn began to brighten in the east. Only a little time remained before the hue and cry would begin, and he must find a place of concealment before then, else he were lost. Pomponio knew every part of the forests for miles around; and after getting under cover of them, he turned at a slight angle toward the southwest, and made straight for a cave he had once visited when hunting for a bear. He remembered it was concealed by a thick tangled mass of bushes and young trees, hiding it so effectually that discovery was well nigh impossible. In pursuing the bear, Pomponio had tracked it to the cave which it had entered, and this it was that gave him the secret. Summoning all his remaining strength for a last supreme effort, he dragged himself on slowly and painfully. It was not far, and soon he recognised the clump of bushes that shaded the entrance; and none too soon, for just before reaching it, he heard a musket shot in the direction of the presidio. His flight was discovered. But he was safe, for the present, at least; and crouching down in the depths of the dark cave, kind nature once more came to his relief, and he knew no more.

Great was the excitement at the presidio when Pomponio's escape was discovered. The soldiers, on going past the place on their morning rounds, saw the bloody tracks of the prisoner's descent on the wall under the window. An instant investigation was made, and the truth of the awful manner in which Pomponio had accomplished his evasion disclosed. Stupefied, the commandant and his men gazed at the traces of the deed, the pools of half-dried dark blood and the two pieces of bone, eloquent of the fortitude he must have possessed, the desperation he was in, to perpetrate such an act.

Might not it be thought that so astonishing a hardihood would have awakened a feeling of admiration and pity for the unfortunate being? So heroic a deed would have elicited praise to rend the skies from the peoples of antiquity,* and the story of Pomponio would have passed down from generation to generation as that of one of their brave men. But, alas! in the breasts of the men with whom Pomponio had to deal, no such sentiment of ruth was raised. On the contrary, they were roused to an even greater violence of hatred and anger toward the poor savage. Wild with rage that his prisoner, whom he had hunted for so long, should have escaped when securely bound, the commandant sent out his men in squads of four and five to scour the woods and find their prey. "He must and shall be found," he said.

The search was instituted forthwith. For days, weeks and months, they hunted for Pomponio, but not a trace of him was found. Gradually, as time

*"*Un trait que les Anciens auraient divinisè.*" Duhaut-Cilly.

went on, the search was given up, for the intense excitement roused by his flight died out from want of fresh fuel to feed upon, and, in addition, the soldiers were required for other more immediate needs; so that, before a year was past after his escape, all interest in the subject ceased, and Pomponio was seldom thought of, or his name spoken, except among those of the Indians to whom he and his deed were ever an impulse toward insubordination.

And what was Pomponio doing? At first from necessity, on account of his wounded feet, and afterward so long as the soldiers kept up a vigorous search for him, he made the cave, in which he had taken refuge, his home. All that day, following the night of his escape, he lay in the cave, more dead than alive, caring for nothing, wishing, even, he might die, now he was out of the grasp of his enemies. But the next morning the pangs of hunger awakened him to life and its realities. Nearly two days were passed since he had had a morsel to eat. He was too weak to go in search of food, and his only help must come from making his presence known to some of the Indians who were scattered in the forest. Pomponio crawled to the opening, and out beyond the clump of bushes hiding it, with the greatest caution. Slowly and painfully he reconnoitred in every direction—no trace or sound of the soldiers. Picking out a vantage point, from which he had a survey among the trees of several hundred feet radius, he took up his watch, keeping a careful lookout for the soldiers, as well as for any of his kindred who might chance to wander thither. Here he passed the day, his little strength slowly leaving him as the hours went by, until, near evening, he felt that unless help came before the darkness fell, he could not survive the night. Almost past caring whether the soldiers found him, he lay back against a little heap of leaves he had scooped together, giving himself up to the numb, delicious feeling of the last sleep—no more to be feared and fought against—when his ear caught the sound of steps, muffled by the leaves of the undergrowth carpeting the ground. He started; life for an instant returned to him. Did that portend the approach of the soldiers, or was it some friendly Indian roaming the forest for game, and now on his return home? He gazed into the obscurity of the approaching night, lying back too weak to move, though it were his enemies come to take him again. But his fear was vain. It was an Indian boy, not more than fifteen years old, on the way to his tribe. At sight of him Pomponio was rejoiced, for the nearing Indian belonged to his own tribe, and but for his extreme youth would have been included among Pomponio's followers in the contemplated revolt.

His eyes lighted up with the fire of life. He raised himself on an elbow, and when the Indian was within a few yards of him, and about to turn aside to reënter the thicker woods beyond, Pomponio called to him. His voice was hardly above a whisper, but it was sufficient. The Indian heard, and turned quickly. Seeing the form of a man, he started, and was on the point of springing away into the forest, when Pomponio spoke, this time in a louder and stronger tone:

"Help me Taxlipu, I am nearly dead. I am Pomponio."

"Pomponio!" almost shrieked the boy. "It cannot be. I saw Pomponio carried away and locked up at the presidio, and an Indian told me he had been chained fast to the wall of his prison cell."

The boy came nearer as he said this, but he held himself ready to flee at the least movement of the figure lying on the ground. "Surely it is his spirit," he said to himself, "for it is, indeed, the countenance of Pomponio."

But the wounded man spoke again: "I am Pomponio. I cut myself loose from the chains that bound me, and escaped from my prison. Give me a little water, else I die," and again he lost consciousness.

But he was saved. Taxlipu came close, and gazed earnestly at the dark upturned face. Yes, that was Pomponio. He sprang away and dashed madly into the forest, and on to the settlement of the Indians, for help. Here he found a number of Pomponio's followers together, talking sadly of the mishap to their chief. Taxlipu burst in on them with the startling news that Pomponio had escaped and was now in the forest nearly dead. The men sprang up, telling the boy to lead them to the place. But before starting, one of the Indians went to a hut close by, and brought out with him part of a rabbit, freshly cooked, and an *olla* of water. With these, the company set off on the run, led by Taxlipu. It was only a few minutes before they reached the spot where Pomponio lay as one dead. The Indian with the water knelt down by his side, and poured some drops into his mouth. After a short while, during which the dose was repeated as often as it was swallowed, Pomponio opened his eyes, drawing a heavy sigh.

Tenderly and reverently they cared for him. At his request they bore him into the cave where he would be safe from the sight of any chance party from the presidio hunting for him, and here they nursed him back to life and strength. It was many days before he recovered from the effects of the great loss of blood he had suffered; many more before the wounds in his feet healed. From the ill-usage to which he had subjected them, inflammation set in, and at one time great fear was felt that he could not survive; but his strong constitution prevailed. Yet after all he would have died gladly, for he was a helpless cripple from that day, hobbling around only with the aid of rude crutches.

His comrades vied with each other in their attentions to the sick leader, and after he had recovered from the fever and weakness, they furnished him with all the necessaries of life which he was unable to obtain by his own efforts. After a few months in the cave, Pomponio left it to be with the Indians in the forest near the mission; but he was careful to keep away from the neighborhood of the scene of his capture, judging rightly that that place would be under surveillance at any time of uneasiness. However, there was no thought of farther insurrection. Their spirit had been broken with Pomponio's capture, for a long time, at any rate. But although they had abandoned all idea of a general uprising, they did everything in their power to annoy and harass their enemies: stealing their horses and cattle and sheep; devastating their crops of wheat and grapes, and, once or twice, setting fire to an outlying mission house or granary. Their lofty idea of freedom from servitude had degenerated thus into a system of petty depredation.

Here, among his friends, Pomponio passed the days quietly and sadly, caring for nothing, and going through mechanically the routine of each day. His spirit was crushed—not so much from the effects of his treatment, but because his long thought of, long desired, purpose was come to naught. He paid but little attention to the affairs of those about him. They went and came, carried on their game of life, rousing in him only a gleam of interest. Thus three years passed.

One day, in the early spring, the Indians went away on a foraging expedition, leaving Pomponio alone in his hut. It had been a warm, sunny day, and in the afternoon Pomponio dragged himself to a little moss-covered bank under the trees, on which he stretched himself, and, after a short time, he fell asleep. All was quiet. Not a sound was to be heard save the insects humming drowsily in the heated air, and, now and then, the whirr of an oriole as it flew swiftly past, lighting up with a glint of gold the shadows among the trees. The oriole is sunlight incarnate.

But this quiet scene was to be broken. The sound of branches snapping beneath the tread of some heavy foot was heard. It drew near the secluded spot; then the form of a man, carrying a musket, could be discerned, making his way to the glade. He reached the edge of the clearing, when he espied the sleeping Indian, lying with his face turned from him. He halted instantly. Was it an Indian belonging to the mission, and playing truant, or one of the savages of the forests, from whom the mission had suffered so much during the last three years? He must find out. Creeping so slowly and carefully that not a sound was heard again from his feet among the plants, he passed around the edge of the glade to a point nearly opposite, in order to get a more direct view of the sleeping man. What a diabolical expression of alternate hate and triumph passed over his countenance! Here was the scoundrel who had escaped from the presidio. After three years, when hope of cver finding him again had died out, when, except for the depredations continually taking place at the mission and presidio, every one would have declared Pomponio was dead of the wounds he had inflicted on himself, that he, Pablo, the youngest soldier at the presidio, when out hunting, and with no thought of enemies near, should find the miscreant, asleep and in his power! This would advance him in the good graces of the commandant.

There was no time to lose. Pomponio might awake at any moment; his friends in the forest might return on the instant. He raised his musket and took long and steady aim at the Indian. There was a report that raised the echoes. With lightning speed the soldier reloaded, and then cautiously drew nearer; but there was no need of apprehension from Pomponio. He was dead—shot through the heart. The soldier gazed at the inanimate form, at the bullet-hole in his breast, from which the blood was trickling, and at the poor mutilated feet. Did a glimmer of pity stir in his heart? It were hard to say. Yet, as he stood there looking down at his work, perhaps there was a little feeling of sorrow for the fate of his fellow man, coupled with a touch of shame at his own unmanly act in thus murdering his sleeping foe, criminal though he was, and richly deserving death. But he had scant time for reflection. The noise of men approaching was heard in the forest. Pomponio's friends would be here in an instant. He must go at once. He slipped away among the trees in the direction from which he had come, and vanished. A moment later four Indians appeared at the point where the soldier had stood when he fired. Their first glance at Pomponio revealed to them the meaning of the shot they had heard.

Pomponio was buried that night, secretly and in profound silence. His comrades, determined his enemies should never find his grave and body, bore it into the deepest recesses of the forest, and there interred it, afterward removing all trace of any disturbance of the earth covering it. There they left him, at rest, his little part in life's drama ended.

Pablo's story of his killing Pomponio was not believed when he told it at the mission and the presidio. No one, however, could contradict him, and as time went on, and nothing farther was heard of the neophyte, and the marauding at the mission became less, until it ceased altogether, his assertion came, in time, to be regarded as the true account of Pomponio's death.

NOTE.—The writer has taken the liberty of altering the real facts of Pomponio's end. He was captured by a party of four soldiers, tried by court martial at Monterey, in February, and shot, about September, 1824. The period covered by the story, also, has been changed to three years later than the actual time of occurrence. It is surprising that Bancroft, from whose history the facts in this note are taken, does not mention Captain Duhaut-Cilly who, in his *Voyage autour du Monde,* Vol. II, Chap. XI, recounts Pomponio's self-mutilation in order to effect his escape. As Pomponio's execution occurred only three years before Duhaut-Cilly's visit, the French captain must have learned his facts with a close approach to accuracy, and it seems safe to take them without reserve. Bancroft affects to regard the main fact in this story with some incredulity, and limits the victim's manacles to one ankle only. *Vide* Bancroft: *History of California,* Vol. II, pp. 537-38.